Jumper

Michele Martin Bossley

orca sports

Orca Book Publishers

Library and Archives Canada Cataloguing in Publication
Bossley, Michele Martin

Jumper / Michele Martin Bossley.
(Orca sports)

ISBN 10: 1-55143-620-5 / ISBN 13: 978-1-55143-620-3

I. Title. II. Series.
PS8553.O7394J84 2006   jC813'.54   C2006-903486-9

Summary: Reese is determined to save wild horses from the
slaughterhouse.

First published in the United States, 2006
Library of Congress Control Number: 2006929008

Orca Book Publishers gratefully acknowledges the support for its publishing
programs provided by the following agencies: the Government of Canada
through the Book Publishing Industry Development Program and the Canada
Council for the Arts, and the Province of British Columbia through the BC Arts
Council and the Book Publishing Tax Credit.

Cover design by Doug McCaffry
Cover photography by Corbis

ORCA BOOK PUBLISHERS
PO Box 5626, STN. B
VICTORIA, BC CANADA
V8R 6S4

ORCA BOOK PUBLISHERS
PO Box 468
CUSTER, WA USA
98240-0468

www.orcabook.com
Printed and bound in Canada.
11 10 09 08 • 5 4 3 2

For Gigi, who has asked me for years to write a book about horses and show jumping. Here it is, at last.

Other Orca books by Michele Martin Bossley

Swiped

chapter one

"Oh, look, Grandpa! Isn't he—"

"Beautiful. I know, I know," Grandpa interrupted. "You've said that about every horse, Reese."

"But they are. Every single one of them." I leaned against the fence rail to get a better look. Even with the icy raindrops pattering on my face, I couldn't take my eyes off the gelding in front of me. Sixteen hands tall, he took the next jump with a soaring grace that made me catch my breath. "He's fantastic," I whispered. "What I wouldn't give to ride a horse like him.

Grandpa's umbrella wasn't doing a very good job. We were standing out in one of the worst downpours in the history of Spruce Meadows. Spruce Meadows is a famous show-jumping facility just south of Calgary, Alberta, where I live. They hold some of the biggest show-jumping competitions in the world there. My grandfather had gotten tickets for this tournament for my birthday, but it was our bad luck that the competition fell on the same day that southern Alberta was hit with a mammoth rainstorm. Water trickled down the back of my collar, my underwear was uncomfortably damp and my sneakers were soaked, but I didn't care. All I could see was the horse rounding the course in front of me.

Grandpa sneezed, then blew his nose in a tissue. After mopping his face vigorously, he turned to me. "Had enough yet?"

"Oh, please, Grandpa," I begged. "Can't we stay just a little bit longer?"

Grandpa smiled at me, his blue eyes kind. "Well, I'm up to my knees in mud, but I guess I can't get much wetter. A few more minutes won't hurt." He settled his felt cowboy hat a little more firmly over his iron-gray hair.

"Thanks!" I beamed at him. The gelding finished the course to a smattering of applause. Many people had given up and left already. Only those spectators in the covered stands were still dry and comfortable.

The next rider came out on a dancing, skittish mare. She pranced and weaved—I could see the rider was having some trouble controlling her. I watched intensely, trying to pick up the rider's signals to her horse. A good rider's signals are almost undetectable unless you know what to watch for.

The rain had turned the course into a slippery mess, and it was getting worse every second. I could hardly see through the sudden torrent that swept over the field. The mare galloped clumsily through the muck and launched herself toward the first jump. I held my breath as she gathered her forelegs neatly under her body and cleared the poles but landed heavily, hooves splashing in the soggy grass.

"Hey, Gus, couldn't you find a better seat than this?" A man grinned at Grandpa and blew the steam away from his hot cup of coffee. He was around forty-five years old, with thick, dark hair and a rugged, still-handsome face.

"Sitting under a canopy in a cushy chair is for old guys, Jim," Grandpa retorted good-naturedly.

"Rich old guys, you mean," Jim answered. He laughed, but I saw a slight frown crease Grandpa's face.

"Business is good, then," Grandpa said.

"Oh, yeah. Going great, in fact. Between the ranch and the corporate stuff in town, I keep busy all right. I'll tell you, if it weren't for trying to impress clients, I sure wouldn't be out here in this weather. The only good reason for keeping horses is to make money, and jumping them over fences only pays if you're chasing coyotes away from the chickens."

I snapped to attention at that. "These competitions are worth big money, Mr...."

"Bellamy."

"Mr. Bellamy," I finished.

"Yes they are, Missy, but only to the rider who wins. The rest have the cost of keeping an expensive horse in feed, training and vet bills, not to mention travel expenses to competitions. Just so they can jump over a set of pretty poles? Hardly worth it."

"Depends on who you're talking to," I said, stung by the nickname Missy. Who did this guy think he was, anyway? "I happen to think training horses as beautiful as these is worth a lot more than money," I continued.

Jim Bellamy's green eyes narrowed. I don't think people disagreed with him to often. "You might change your mind about that someday, when your mommy and daddy don't pay your bills for you."

My face flamed. Bellamy turned to Grandpa. "See you around, Gus." He strode off to the covered seats, his coffee still sending up wisps of steam.

"What a total jerk!" I burst out as soon as he was out of earshot. Grandpa glanced at me. "Well, he is! Who says he can call me Missy and criticize show jumping? Show jumping is amazing, and he can just stuff it!"

Grandpa suppressed a grin with difficulty. "Jim Bellamy has a ranch down the road a ways from mine. I've known him for years. He's always said what he wants and the heck with what everybody else thinks."

"Really?" I said coldly. "Well, maybe someone should remind him that there is such a thing as manners."

"Maybe someone should," Grandpa agreed. He paused in thought. "Maybe you just did."

"Not enough," I said grumpily. The rain was still coming down in torrents. The next horse and rider were consulting with some Spruce Meadows officials. I wondered if they might call off the rest of the competition, but it didn't matter much anymore. I was wet and cold, and the rest of the show was ruined for me. I glanced at Grandpa's mud-covered boots. "Come on, Grandpa. Let's go home."

chapter two

"No, NO! Push him forward! Put pressure on your outside leg as you round the turn. Straighten his head, Reese!" Laurel, my coach, yelled across the ring as Dublin approached the fence too close to one side and refused the jump. He stopped so abruptly I nearly lost my balance in the saddle. "You need to give him the right aids," Laurel called from her seat on an old chuck wagon in the center of the arena. "Squeeze with your legs on the stride before the jump. The timing has to be split-second!"

I wiped the sweat from my forehead with the back of my wrist and readjusted my helmet, tucking wisps of my brown hair back inside. "Okay. We'll try it again." I reached forward and patted Dublin's smooth neck. "Come on, Dub. You can do it," I encouraged. Dublin snorted, shifting the bit in his mouth.

I was at my Saturday riding lesson, putting Dublin over the jumps in the indoor ring. The arena's dirt floor, covered in a thick layer of sand mixed with ground-up rubber tire chips, made the air smell dusty-sweet and muffled the sound in the open space. Three of the other girls in my class were waiting for their turn at the jumps.

I circled Dublin and headed for our last fence. I leaned forward, urging him on as I counted his strides. When we were less than three away from the jump, I loosened the reins and rose in the saddle, shifting my weight to help Dublin with the takeoff. I squeezed hard with my legs and felt his body bunch, then stretch, beneath me as we soared through space. It was the most glorious, floating feeling, but the earth rushed to meet us too quickly, and Dublin's front hooves hit the dirt with a thud. I jolted a bit in the saddle and had to gather the reins quickly or I would have lost control of the horse.

I let Dublin canter for a few paces before I started to slow him down, bringing him around to where Laurel was standing.

She frowned. "That landing needs work," she said.

"I know. I didn't have time to get ready. He was so quick."

"I think we should do some flatwork. You and Dublin are a bit off on your rhythm, and I think that's what is causing the problem." Laurel put her hands on both hips and studied me. "I think you could use some fine-tuning. Sometimes making small adjustments makes a big difference. We'll work on that next time. Cool him down, then go ahead and untack. I think Dublin's done for the day."

I nodded and swung down from the saddle. I took hold of the reins and walked Dublin around the outside edge of the ring a few times before I led him to the big double doors at the far end of the arena. I paused to watch the other girls as I slid one door open. Kayla Richards was heading for the first jump on her horse, Twilight, with a gait so smooth they looked like they were cantering in slow motion.

I swallowed and turned away. Riding was so much harder than it looked. It wasn't fair. People thought that you just climbed up into the saddle and away you went, but there was a lot more to it than that.

I led Dublin into the short passageway from the arena to the stable and over to his stall, which was one of the closest ones to the arena doors. I could still hear Laurel yelling faintly, but it seemed to me she sounded a lot more positive than she had with me.

I sighed. Tethering Dublin loosely to the gatepost by his reins, I grabbed a bucket of brushes from the nearby supply room.

"You really are a stubborn old goat," I told him. He tossed his head at the disapproval in my voice, but I didn't care. "Why can't you just *behave*?" I lifted the flap of the saddle, unbuckled the girth and scooted around him to unbuckle the other side, sliding the saddle from his sweaty back. I stored it in one of the stable's lockers and hung the saddle pads up to dry.

"You're a darn nuisance, even if you are good-looking." I kept talking as I grabbed the currycomb and began to brush the sweat from his back in swift, firm circles. He whickered in what I thought sounded like a pleased way. "But looks aren't everything," I answered sternly. I took a soft brush and leaned into his flank, brushing the dust from his coat. Dublin was a bay, which means he was a deep brown all over, with darker legs. He had white socks on all his feet and a white blaze on his forehead. His mane and tail were black. Dublin nosed at the pockets of my coat as I worked my way forward, bending down to brush away the sweat where the girth had been tightened.

"There's no carrots in there, big guy," I told him. "You'll just have to wait."

Dublin responded by blowing his nose into the folds of my jacket. "Hey!" I stepped back as he snorted again. "All right, Mr. Greedy. Just one for now." I reached into the bag I always brought for my riding equipment and pulled out the carrots. I broke one up and let Dublin take it from my hand, stroking the side of his face as he nosed my palm. He crunched it quickly and looked immediately for more, but I had the hoof pick and I pulled up on his right front foot. He grudgingly lifted his foot so I could scrape out all the dirt and crud that accumulates during a ride. When it was clean, I let him go and grabbed his hind foot. I tugged, but Dublin refused to budge. "Oh, come *on*," I said. Tug. Tug.

"Fine," I huffed. I reached into the bag of carrots and let him have another one. He let me lift his hind foot, and I cleaned it as quickly as I could, but when I went on to the next hind leg, we went through the same performance again. Tug. Tug.

"You know, you could be sold," I said, my hands on my hips.

"But not to you." Kayla led Twilight through the big double doors just in time to hear my comment.

"What's that supposed to mean?" I swung around. I nearly added "rich girl" to the end of that sentence, but decided against it. I didn't want to fight with her.

"Nothing," Kayla answered snidely, tying Twilight to the post at his stall. She took off her helmet, stripped the elastic from her short, pale blond braids and shook out her hair. I hated to admit it, but Kayla was pretty, in a trendy, cool kind of way. She made me feel ugly. If I braided my frizzy brown hair, I'd look like I had sticks growing from my ears. Kayla's teeth were straight, but if she'd had to wear braces like me, I bet she'd look cute. I looked like I had a mouthful of spare change.

"Are you still planning on moving up to the B Level circuit next year?" Kayla's voice interrupted my thoughts.

I swallowed. I knew right away what Kayla

meant. In order to move up from the Novice Development circuit to the B Level circuit, a rider had to lease or own their horse. Right now, Dublin was just my lesson horse. Even though I rode him every weekend, he wasn't really mine, and a bunch of other students rode him during the week. The problem was, owning a horse is expensive. Very expensive. And buying a top-quality jumper is more expensive yet. Some horses that are trained for show jumping can cost more than $20,000. Add vet bills, all the tack, feed, stable fees for boarding—well, I didn't even want to think about it. My mom and dad couldn't afford to buy me a horse. Even leasing a horse was out of the question. Lessons were about all we could afford, which meant I'd probably be stuck in the Novice Development circuit forever.

Unlike Kayla, whose parents were loaded. Kayla owned Twilight and could pay for the best feed, a fancy saddle and the best riding clothes. She never let me forget it, either.

"I'll move up when I can get a horse. And

when I do, it won't be because I didn't have enough talent to get there," I retorted.

Kayla's face burned red. She led Twilight to his stall without a word. Even though Twilight was a great horse and made the jumps look effortless, Kayla wasn't consistent enough on him for Laurel to move Kayla up.

Mind you, I wasn't consistent either. Dublin was such a strong-willed horse. I sighed for a second time and slapped Dublin on the rump. "Get your big butt over," I said. Dublin moved so I could squeeze by him and loosen the reins. I loved Dublin, but he challenged me every single time I rode him. It would sure be nice if I could have a horse whose personality meshed with mine, one who would be a friend, instead of one who tested me every step of the way.

"Yeah, keep dreaming," I muttered as I led Dublin into his stall.

chapter three

"Grandpa, STOP!" I hollered.

My grandfather hit the brakes, and the truck slid to a grinding stop on the muddy road.

"What's the matter? Did the tractor come loose?" Grandpa craned his neck to see out the back window of the truck. We were towing in an old tractor that had coughed and died in the fields more than two weeks earlier. Grandpa had a friend who could fix it for a lot less money than a regular mechanic, but he lived on a farm southeast of Calgary. I was spending Saturday afternoon with Grandpa, so we had driven out to the field, hitched the tractor to the back of the truck and were now towing it on a trailer.

"No, look!" I pointed off into the distance. Along the ridge a group of horses was running. The late afternoon sun glinted off their backs, almost silhouetting them against the empty sky. "How cool is that?" I breathed in awe.

"Those might be the wild horses. The ones that are causing so much trouble on the military land."

I looked at him. "What wild horses?"

"Haven't you heard about them? That band of horses has been running wild for years now. Most of 'em used to be owned, but they got away somehow and they've been breeding and living on the grasslands for a few generations. The military's got some bee in its bonnet about the horses damaging the ecosystem, and there's talk about rounding them up."

"What will they do with them?" I asked.

Grandpa shrugged. "I don't know. Sell them maybe."

I watched the horses turn away from the ridge and start heading toward us. "Can we walk to the fence? Get a better look at them?" I asked.

"Reese, I want to get this tractor dropped off so we can get back to the ranch before supper."

"Please?"

Grandpa sighed. "Oh, all right. Let's go." He pulled over onto the grassy roadside, opened the door of the truck with a creak and stepped out into mud. "Watch out," he warned as I opened my own door and nearly fell into a bush.

We traipsed through the grass, the autumn sunlight the only warmth. The wind was cold, the ground slick and icy from the rains that had turned to sleet overnight. The horses couldn't smell us; we were walking into the wind, so they didn't turn and run when we reached the fence.

The horses slowed to a trot. Then, finding a new patch of grass, most stopped to graze. I watched them with interest. There were a few that looked like yearlings, and several were foals that stayed by their mothers. The rest looked fully grown, shaggy with their new growth of winter coat. I could see a young mare dancing sideways, playing with another horse that nipped at her. She was a deep red chestnut; her coat had a burnished look in the sun. She lifted her head, and for one moment she stared right at me. Her overgrown mane whipped in the wind, but otherwise she was perfectly still. I didn't move, didn't even breathe, but the wind veered, the horses caught our scent, and they began to trot away. The mare cantered ahead, jumped a pile of logs and bracken, then coaxed her playmate to race her, thundering ahead of the band.

"Did you see that?" I said to Grandpa. "That mare jumped those logs like they were nothing!" I knew untrained horses almost never jump—they'd rather go around obstacles if they can.

"She's a natural, all right," Grandpa agreed. His seamed face relaxed in a smile. "Now you just have to catch her."

I snorted. "Good luck."

There was a soft thrum of hooves, and several more horses burst over the ridge. Something was wrong. This was no playful gallop but a flat-out run. The other horses pricked their ears, immediately on edge, ready to run.

Far away, I heard a chugging, metallic sound. The two groups of horses joined, and the herd streaked across the prairie toward us, away from that noise. Panic was etched in their every movement, from the frightened eyes to the straining limbs. They thundered past, near the fence line, nearly close enough for me to touch. I could smell sweat and dust as they passed.

The red chestnut trailed the band. She didn't look as frightened as some of the mustangs, but she ran behind them in a resigned sort of way. She skimmed by the fence. Without thinking, I put out my hand. She shied and summoned a burst of speed—in less than a second she caught up with the herd, fighting her way in among the ranks. Man, she was fast. I watched them go.

"What spooked them?" I asked.

"Sounded like tanks. The soldiers are out here training, after all."

"Would they shoot them?" The thought horrified me.

"No. But those horses are probably a bit of a nuisance. I imagine that the military would like to be well rid of them."

"Is that why they're going to round them up?"

"No. Apparently the land is getting damaged by the bands of horses roaming out here," Grandpa said.

I stared after the horses as they grew smaller in the distance. "They sure are beautiful though, running free like that. I wonder what it would be like to ride one of them."

Grandpa looked at his watch. "Come on, Reese. If I'm ever going to get that tractor fixed, we'd better get going."

"Okay." I turned back toward the truck, stepping carefully over the sludge and tangled grass, but I couldn't get my mind off that chestnut mare. As Grandpa let out the clutch on the truck and we bumped carefully back onto the road, I kept turning the same thoughts over in my mind.

If I could catch her, could I break her? And more importantly, could I train her to jump?

chapter four

"So Dublin will be gone tomorrow, then?" I heard Kayla's voice from inside Twilight's stall.

"The new owners will be here in the morning." Laurel handed Kayla a hoof pick over the half wall.

I stopped dead, dropping a bucket of grooming tools with a clatter on the stable floor. Twilight skittered at the noise, jerking at his lead rope. Kayla had to grab the halter with both hands to keep him calm. She glared in my direction.

"Sorry," I said. "But what was that about Dublin?"

"He's been sold," Laurel answered.

"When were you going to tell me?" The sharpness of the loss hit me like a blow.

"Today," Laurel replied evenly.

"So I just show up for a lesson and Dublin's gone? I've been training on that horse for months!" My face stung. I always knew Dublin didn't belong to me, but I felt as though he did. We were like partners.

"Reese, Dublin was on loan to us. If someone wants to buy him, he's for sale. You know that. Better go tack up. You'll be riding Boots today."

Kayla's expression melted into a tiny, smug smile. She began to currycomb Twilight, but I could see she was listening.

"Boots!" My stomach sank with dismay. I thought Dublin had been stubborn, but he was an angel compared with Boots. Boots was the oldest horse the stable had. She was well named—she had the personality of an old boot and the looks to match. I wouldn't care about that except that I had no chemistry with her at all. If there was a rider who could get her to jump, it wasn't me, and I was trying to prepare for a competition. How was I supposed to compete on an old nag like that?

"Boots is a good horse. She's a solid jumper and she knows the ropes. You'll do just fine on her," Laurel said firmly, obviously guessing what I was thinking. "Besides, there's no other horse available right now."

I swallowed. It was Boots or nothing. So just like that, my chances of winning in the next show were in the toilet. Even if Laurel had handed me the best jumper in the world, it would be difficult to get ready in time with a new horse—but with Boots? Forget it. No wonder Kayla looked so smug. I picked up the currycombs and brushes I'd dropped and tossed them in the bucket with more force than was really necessary. Then I marched down the row of stalls without a backward glance. Kayla didn't need to know how I felt.

Boots stuck her nose over the half wall as I approached. Her coat was gray and speckled, her dark mane wispy. She laid back her ears at my grumpy expression. I swear, horses know what you're thinking before you've even thought it. She knew I intended to saddle her up, and she knew I wasn't looking forward to it. She was already shifting her rump in front of the gate to make it harder for me to get inside.

I sighed and dug into my pocket. Holding the carrot out to her, I let her smell me and take the treat. She crunched it thoughtfully, as if to say that bribery might help, but I still hadn't won her over.

"Move," I said, slapping her hindquarters. She sidestepped away from me and let me in the stall. I haltered her and led her out, tethering her to the gate before I grabbed a hoof pick. She let me lift her feet and clean the hooves, but it was when I had worked my way around to her other foreleg that she made her move. My bum was nicely exposed when I bent over. She nipped me hard with her blunt, yellow teeth.

"Yowch!" I yelped. It felt like someone had pinched me with a pair of pliers, and I stood up in hurry. I clapped a hand over my backside and glared at her. I wanted to smack that horse a good one, but of course I couldn't do that. If you want an animal to trust you, walloping it isn't a good idea, even if it is an ornery old mule of a horse. Instead I grabbed the halter and gave it a small, fierce shake. "Don't you ever do that again, you walking reject from the glue factory!" I fixed Boots with the most menacing stare I could muster. Then I let go of the halter and rubbed my backside. "Rotten horse," I muttered. I tacked her up as quickly as I could and led her to the arena.

The other kids in my riding lesson were already there. Kayla was waiting with Twilight, who looked more beautiful and docile than ever, I noticed bitterly.

"Everything okay?" Kayla asked. "I heard a yell from over there. What happened?"

"Nothing. Everything's just fine," I said through gritted teeth. I swung up into the saddle. All I wanted to do was get through the lesson. I could be riding an elephant at this point and it wouldn't matter.

"All right, ladies," Laurel called as we entered the arena. "We're doing flatwork today. You can all use some polishing, and Reese needs the opportunity to work with Boots before attempting a jump, so I'd like you to warm up. Then we'll start with leg yielding."

Leg yielding is when you instruct the horse to move with his body on a diagonal. That might seem weird, but it's useful for two reasons: one, to keep your horse supple; and two, to make sure he's listening to you and obeying instructions.

I adjusted my helmet and gave Boots the signal to trot. She began smoothly and carried me around the ring. Surprisingly, I found her gait quite easy to post to, and we finished the warm-up without a problem. I had half-suspected that Boots might toss me off, but when Laurel called to begin the leg yielding down the long wall, Boots obeyed my signals without complaint.

"I need to see a bit more angle from a few of you," Laurel hollered from her seat in the arena. "Reese, that's not bad. Make sure you're holding your position. Now look for your diagonal." Laurel watched for a few minutes without comment. "Good job, folks. Let's move on to downward transitions. Let's ride a few canter-trot transitions. What you want to be thinking about during these transitions is using your legs."

I began to relax. Boots was doing better than I expected. I signaled her to canter and she speeded up immediately. But when I gave her the direction to slow to a trot, she didn't stop but barreled on ahead.

"Whoa!" I hissed at her, signaling harder. Boots reluctantly dropped to a trot, tossing her head in defiance.

"Boots needs to be a bit rounder on that trot, Reese." Laurel watched me carefully.

I wrestled with the horse, but she refused to pay attention to my signals and trotted however she wanted.

"She's not listening to you," Laurel yelled. "And she's being a bit rude about it."

"I know!" I answered in exasperation.

"I want you to stop. Make her halt, wait, back up four steps, then trot," Laurel called.

I tried, but Boots was difficult, shaking her head and backing up only slightly before trying to move forward again.

"Tap her with your crop," Laurel said.

I moved to grab the whip, but Boots knew exactly what I was going to do. With a quick backward kick, she tossed me out of the saddle and into the soft dirt. Landing on my already-sore backside, I unclipped my helmet and threw it down in frustration. I knew I could kiss my chances of placing at the Greenbriar Invitational goodbye. As I stared at Boots, the image of that wild mare with her chestnut coat gleaming red in the sun rose up in front of my eyes. And suddenly I wanted her more than anything else I had ever wanted in my entire life.

chapter five

"Honey, I'm really sorry." Mom stopped peeling potatoes and leaned against the counter. "I know moving up to the next division is really important to you, but Dad and I just can't handle the cost of leasing a horse. There's a lot more to it than just the price tag on the animal—and you know that a good jumper isn't cheap."

"I know," I said.

"There are vet bills and feed and boarding the horse." Dad put the stack of plates he

31

was carrying down on the kitchen table. "It's very expensive."

"I know," I repeated miserably. After my disastrous lesson on Boots, I was hoping that I might be able to lease a horse—the stable usually had several horses available, and it would be a way for me to move up a level next season *and* get away from Boots.

"I just don't see how we could do it," Mom continued.

"If I were able to get a horse cheap and board it at Grandpa's after the competition season, would we be able to afford that?" I asked.

Mom frowned in thought. "Well, maybe. That would help with some of the expenses, but where are you going to get a trained show jumper for a low cost? That just doesn't happen, Reese."

"Maybe not." I sighed. Laurel had stopped me after the lesson and told me that even though I was having trouble with Boots, she still wanted me to compete on her at the Invitational. I didn't think that was such a hot idea—after all, she had already tossed me off once, but Laurel insisted that we'd be fine after a few more lessons.

Dad rubbed a hand through his thinning gray hair, making it stand out like a wire brush. "Besides, it's not really a big deal. You're such a good rider, I'm sure you'll do great on this new horse once you get used to her."

I closed my eyes. Dad knew basically nothing about show jumping. He was much more involved with my two younger brothers' hockey teams than my riding. I had no doubt that part of the reason we couldn't afford to lease a horse was because every year we had a whopping bill for hockey fees, skates, equipment, sticks and tournaments. I didn't resent that—my little brothers were great skaters and they had as much right as I did to want to do something they loved. It's just that Dad seemed to think horses were a hobby, not something really important. So he didn't blink when it came to paying for extra ice time for Drew and Liam, but new tack or boots or something always took some persuasion.

"You don't understand," I complained. "This isn't a horse. It's an old nag! I may as well try jumping with a donkey."

"Well, a donkey would definitely be less expensive," Dad tried to joke. Then he saw my face, set in a stubborn frown. "You may as well stop whining, Reese. There's nothing we can do about it."

"I know that!" I bit back an angry retort. It would help if my parents shared my passion for riding, but since they didn't, I would have to figure this problem out on my own.

"I don't know if we can find them, Reese." Grandpa bumped the truck along the back-country road. "If the mustangs are deep in the military land, we'll never spot them from the road."

"Can't we drive onto the military base?"

"No," Grandpa said. "It's restricted access."

"Don't you know someone who could let us in?" I persisted.

Grandpa chuckled. "I'm not a magician, you know." He glanced over at me. "This is really important to you, isn't it?"

"Yes." I couldn't explain it. There was just something about that red chestnut mare that I couldn't forget. Part of me knew logically that buying one of the wild mustangs was probably the only way I could ever afford to own my own horse, but the other part of me wanted that horse just because. Because she was fast. Because she was beautiful. Because in that split second that our eyes had met, I felt a connection with her that I'd never felt with any other horse, not even Dublin.

"Look! There they are," I cried, pointing to a group of horses grazing in a small gully. Grandpa glanced in the direction I was pointing. I gripped the edge of my seat as we hit a rut in the road. The truck gave a tremendous clank, and Grandpa jerked the steering wheel to one side. The truck bucked like a farting bull, then wobbled to the side of the road.

"Uh-oh. Looks like we've got a flat," Grandpa said. He guided the limping truck to a stop, then opened the door. "This could take a few minutes, Reese. I haven't changed a tire on this old truck in years."

"That's okay." I looked around. "Is it all right if I have a look for the horses?"

"Sure. Just stay away from the fences." Grandpa pulled a toolbox from the back of the truck.

I climbed up the embankment, taking care to stay away from the barbed wire that enclosed the military base. The land stretched away from me, a smooth, rolling surface. I glanced over my shoulder, but Grandpa was still wrestling with the lug nuts on the tire.

"Need some help?" I called back.

Grandpa waved me off. "No, it's all right. They're just a little tight. I'll get it."

I nodded and started walking along the fence line. The truck grew smaller in the distance as I walked farther. I felt entirely alone, even knowing Grandpa was there, with that vast prairie stillness surrounding me.

The horses were much closer now. I could see them, but the barbed wire fence prevented me from getting near enough to really get a good look. I studied the fence.

Grandpa had told me to stay away from it. He hadn't specifically said I couldn't go through it. I glanced back. Grandpa was still working on the truck—his back was to me. There were some bushes and tall grasses that helped hide me a little.

I took a deep breath, lifted the bottom wire and wriggled underneath it. Facedown, I could smell the dusty, sunbaked grass and the earthy scent of the damp soil. My shirt was getting smudged with it. I dug my knees into the dirt and dragged myself under the fence.

The horses were watching me, their eyes alert, ears pricked. I saw the red chestnut mare standing near a wild rose bush, munching some still-green grass that had been sheltered by the bush. She eyed me thoughtfully. I took careful, slow steps toward her.

"Hey, pretty girl," I said softly. "You're sure beautiful, aren't you?"

The mare gave a snort and ambled out of the rose bush, moving leisurely away from me as I came closer. I stood still and held out my hand. The rest of the horses were edgy. They gradually backed into a nervous clump and watched the mare uneasily.

The mare lifted her nose. Her nostrils widened as she caught my unfamiliar scent. Slowly, I reached into my jacket pocket and pulled out the carrots I'd brought. I didn't know if I could tempt her—wild horses would never come near a person, carrots or no carrots. But Grandpa had told me that some of these horses used to be tame. The mare didn't really seem afraid of me, which made me wonder if she used to belong to someone.

She stretched her neck out, but it was hard for her to investigate the carrots in my hand from twenty feet away. She took a cautious step forward. I held my breath.

An angry squeal erupted from the far side of the band. A mighty head shot up, ears pricked, eyes fiery wild. My heart gave a great frightened thud. The stallion had apparently decided he didn't like what we were up to and was not shy about letting me know.

I backed away. He circled the band, drawing them into a tighter ring, contemplating me all the while. I backed away faster. I was only ten feet away from the fence when the stallion charged. I bolted for the fence and dove under, the barbs catching on my shirt, scraping my back. I wiggled frantically, but the barbs caught on the belt of my jeans and held fast. The stallion's hooves pounded against the ground. I tried to roll sideways to loosen the barbs, struggling to get most of my body underneath the fence. I knew that the stallion could still reach me, though. He could kick or trample me—those hooves would pummel me to a pulp.

I looked up in terror as the enormous creature pounded toward me and I fought to get under the wire, thrashing my legs, yanking the wire upward.

The red chestnut mare bolted suddenly, right into the stallion's path. He reared to avoid hitting her, clouds of dust billowing up as he twisted and plunged sideways. She streaked away from him across the prairie. Distracted from his goal of cutting me to pieces, the stallion shot after his runaway mare at a furious gallop. She squealed as he sank his teeth into her flank and turned her back toward the band.

I pushed upward on the wire with all my strength. There was a ripping noise as the cloth finally gave way and I rolled to safety on the other side of the fence.

Sort of.

Grandpa was striding toward me, outraged disbelief on his face. "Reese!" he shouted. I cringed as he grabbed my arm, hauling me to my feet. "What were you thinking!" he bellowed. "You could have been killed!" Without waiting for an answer, he wrapped me in a hug so tight I could barely breathe. I could feel Grandpa's heart hammering against his ribs, and instantly I knew that he had been really scared.

"I'm sorry, Grandpa," I said, my voice muffled in his shirt.

Grandpa released me and swallowed hard. "Are you all right?"

I nodded, but I realized as I did that at least half a dozen places on my body stung badly, my shirt was torn to ribbons and stained with dirt and my own blood, and my hands were red with welts from the wire. "It hurts a bit," I admitted.

"I have some iodine that I keep in the truck. I'll paint you up, and that'll hold you till we get home." Grandpa headed back in the direction of the truck.

As I hobbled after him, I glanced back at the herd of mustangs. The chestnut mare had managed to evade any more punishment from the stallion, and once she was back in the band, he seemed satisfied. The stallion was moving the herd up the gully and over the ridge, deeper into the military's land.

Grandpa rummaged in the glove compartment and found an ancient bottle of iodine. I set my teeth as he dabbed it on the worst of the scratches.

"This is gonna hurt," Grandpa warned. I nearly howled as he painted the deep cut on my lower back where the barbed wire had caught in my now-tattered jeans.

"Why do you suppose she did that?" I gasped through the stinging pain.

"Who did what?" Grandpa said, capping the bottle. "All done."

"The mare. Running past the stallion like that. She probably saved my life."

"I know," Grandpa said soberly. "For one terrible minute I thought you wouldn't make it. I was trying to get there first, but I'm no match for a charging stallion." Grandpa paused.

I didn't want to think about it anymore. "Let's go home," I said.

chapter six

"Next rider in the ring, number 81, Taylor Jennings on Fraggle Rock." The announcer's voice boomed over the loudspeakers.

I peeked into the arena. It was similar to ours, but Greenbriar's jumps had all been decorated with pots of silk flowers for the competition. It looked colorful and festive—a lot different from the usual training ring.

I adjusted my paper number carefully so it wouldn't rip. It was tied with narrow, dark-colored string over my riding jacket. I was used to the uniform riders used for shows now, but I still remembered how I felt when I went to my first jumping competition. Everyone looked so different. We always wore beige breeches and high, polished boots, but the tailored dark jackets, white blouses and velvet helmets made the riders seem so formal and impressive—I could hardly believe it was us.

Just outside the ring, Kayla was finishing the complicated job of plaiting Twilight's mane. His coat shone. Even his hooves were polished. Kayla herself looked sophisticated with her glossy, blond hair pulled back in a low knot at her neck. Her jacket fitted perfectly, and a chunky gold pin held her collar closed.

I tugged self-consciously at the sleeves of my own jacket, which were getting too short. My hair was French-braided into two pigtails behind my ears, but curly wisps were escaping everywhere. I looked like a mad scientist, but I didn't have time to redo the braids. I just stuffed my helmet on and went to the stall where they'd put Boots. She was still blanketed, but I'd brought my saddle with me, along with the big plastic container with all my riding stuff. It was right where I left it, outside the stall, but when I began to tack up, I noticed my martingale was missing. I shuffled the saddle blanket to one side, picked up my gloves, brushes, the bridle—but no martingale.

I couldn't ride without it. A martingale helps the rider control the horse by limiting how high the horse can lift his head, and it was important. I knew I'd brought it. I'd double-checked all my equipment at home.

" Everything all right?" said Kayla's voice at my elbow.

I whirled, startling Boots. "No. Not really," I answered bluntly. "My martingale is missing."

"Oh. Well, Laurel said to tell you to hurry up. Our class is starting in ten minutes."

I felt a flash of annoyance. "Great. Except that I can't ride without a martingale. Have *you* seen it anywhere?"

Kayla caught my tone and stared at me, unblinking. "No. Why would I?"

"Oh, I don't know. Maybe to make sure that I can't compete."

Kayla smirked. "Why would I bother? You hardly have a chance riding this horse. I wouldn't waste my time." With that, she turned on her heel and stalked away.

My face flamed. Why had I said that? Kayla and I definitely weren't friends, but I had no reason to think she would cheat. Besides, she was right. If she *was* going to risk sabotaging my equipment, it would be smarter to do it for a competition that I might actually *win*.

I quickly threw the saddle blanket on Boots, then put the saddle on and tightened the girth. I rummaged in the container for my hoof pick, and it was when I tossed aside my spare coat—the one I wear over my riding jacket in the stable after I compete—that the martingale fell out. It had gotten hooked inside somehow, and when I had crumpled the jacket up and shoved it inside the container, I guess I hadn't noticed it.

Now I really felt bad. My spirits low, I picked out Boots's hooves and finished tacking up. Laurel came striding up the corridor.

"Reese, come on! Your class is starting," she called.

I led Boots toward the ring. Kayla was mounted on Twilight, trying to keep him calm. She leaned down and patted his neck, whispering something.

I walked toward her. "I found the martingale," I said.

Kayla frowned. "Good for you."

"I'm sorry." I looked at her steadily. "I shouldn't have made it sound like you took it. Good luck out there." I turned Boots around, went to my place in line and mounted up. I could feel Kayla staring after me, and I wouldn't have put it past her to have her mouth open in surprise. I didn't think we'd ever said anything nice to one another. I wasn't really sure why. Sometimes people just don't connect.

Boots shifted under my weight. I leaned forward. "You'll do great. Just listen to me, okay?" She flicked her ears in my direction.

The wait took forever. I couldn't see how Kayla did, but she slid off Twilight when it was over, her face beaming and flushed with exertion. Laurel stopped her and gave her some instructions for the next round, gesturing emphatically with her hands. Kayla nodded, then led Twilight away.

There were two more riders in front of me. Then one more. I took a deep breath.

"Next rider in the ring, number 64, Reese Drayton on Puss 'N' Boots."

I nudged Boots forward and began to canter her toward the first jump. I was desperately trying to remember the order of the course. That's one of the challenges—they change the order of the jumps at every competition, so you always have to memorize a new sequence. If you forget and take a jump out of turn, you are eliminated.

We were approaching the first jump. I counted the strides under my breath. One... two...three...I gave Boots the signal, but she took off a little late. I heard the soft clunk of her back hooves hitting the poles. I dared not look behind to see if the pole fell.

Instead, I focused on the next jump. Boots fought for her head, shaking it irritably as I held her under control. Her canter was rough—

I could feel it jolting beneath me. I let her have a looser rein and used my legs more, trying to smooth her out, but she still pranced, dodging away from the floral arrangement set up at the far end of the ring as we circled toward jump number two. I urged her forward, but I could tell before we even got there that her heart wasn't in it. She stopped short a few feet away, nearly shooting me over her head. I hung on, feeling the blood rush to my face. The refusal would mean I would lose points. If she did it again, I'd be disqualified.

In Novice, it was okay for your trainer to instruct you during your ride, and I heard Laurel's voice, a thin call from the other end of the ring. "Reese, use the crop!"

I gritted my teeth and gripped the whip in my fist. "Darn mule," I whispered. I tapped Boots sharply on the flank with my crop, and she leapt forward, her canter smooth and quick. I turned her toward jump number three. She took it with ease, which made me madder. She could have jumped the other two if she'd wanted to—she was just showing me who was boss.

"Not anymore," I said. I held the reins lightly and used my legs for control. Boots went over the fourth and fifth fences with clean leaps, but on jump number six she balked at the last minute. I squeezed her hard and forced her over, but I could tell she wasn't happy about it.

I guided her around the final circle. She cantered swiftly toward the seventh jump. I tensed in the saddle, ready for the takeoff. One...two...three–!

"Augh!" I squawked as Boots leaned back on her haunches and turned away from the jump. I managed to grab a knot of her mane and clenched my knees into her sides so hard I could hear her grunt, but it was the only thing that prevented me from flying off the horse and into the rails of the fence. As it was, I was so off balance that I slid sideways in the saddle, and it was an easy matter for Boots to give a bouncy little kick and throw me off into the dirt.

I glared at her, then jumped up and snatched the reins before she could take off. The one thing I was *not* going to do was chase my horse around the ring with all these people watching. It was embarrassing enough to be disqualified—with that second refusal, Boots and I were now out—but to be bucked off and then have to catch this ornery animal...

There was a smattering of encouraging applause as I led Boots over to the door into the stable. Laurel tried to stop me as I marched through the sympathetic stares of the other riders, but all I wanted to do was get away.

I still had a second round to jump with Boots. I handed the reins to Laurel. "I quit. I'm not riding this horse."

Laurel stared at me. "You can't do that."

"Oh, yes, I can," I answered grimly. "It's called voluntary withdrawal. I have no hope of placing in the ribbons, and I'm not going to risk another round like that." I turned and walked away.

I found my way to the washroom, where I locked the door and leaned against the wall. The tears came then, and I bawled my heart out for a horse of my own.

chapter seven

"This is it." Grandpa braked on the side of the highway and turned down a dirt road.

I held the crumpled sheet of paper—a notice Grandpa had copied from the bulletin board at the local grocery store—and reread the directions.

"Okay. We're supposed to take the second left and follow the road until we see a barn at the top of the hill," I said.

Grandpa drove around a big pothole, grinding the gears as he shifted down to get up the hill. "This truck's seen better days," he said.

"As long as it can pull the trailer home," I answered with a backward glance at the horse trailer that swayed behind us on the uneven road.

"There's the barn." Grandpa pulled off the road and found a place to park on the grass. I stared with amazement at all the cars, trucks and trailers. They seemed to take up an entire field. I got out and slammed the truck door with a rusty clunk. People were streaming over the grass to a makeshift corral. Beyond the corral there was a huge fenced area where what looked like thousands of horses were bunched, their bodies steaming with sweat in the cold morning sun.

"There are so many," I said, shocked.

"There were quite a few herds of horses running on the military land," said a voice behind me. Grandpa and I turned to see Jim Bellamy, the rancher we'd seen that horrible rainy night at Spruce Meadows. The one who thought horses were useless unless you could make money from them. I wondered what he was doing here. All of these horses were unbroken and would need a lot of work. It seemed a little weird that he would want to buy one.

"I heard that we've got about twelve hundred head up for auction today," Bellamy said jovially.

"Twelve hundred!" I sucked in my breath. How would I ever find the chestnut mare in this crowd?

Grandpa seemed to read my mind. "Come on, Reese. Let's go look for her. Nice to see you, Jim."

Bellamy waved his hand absently, surveying the nearest horses. Grandpa led me over to the fenced area, elbowing gently through other prospective horse buyers until we reached a spot where we could see. I peered anxiously at the milling bodies, trying to pick out a flash of red. Some of the horses looked terrified. Their eyes rolled, showing the whites. Several wheeled out of the crowd and circled, running along the fence, hunting for a way to escape. Dust puffed up under their hooves—already the ground had been pounded to dry dirt.

"There!" Grandpa pointed. "Is that her?"

"Where?" I tried to see. At first there was nothing but a confused mix of gray and brown and black, but then I saw a bit of burnished red, and there she was. I looked closely—there could be more than one red chestnut—but as I watched her move with the same nimble grace I saw out on the prairie, I was sure. There was no room for her to jump, but I was sure that if she could, she'd leap that fence and go. Part of me wished she would. As much as I wanted her, I still wished she could run free.

"That's her," I said, excited. She broke out of the pack, searching the wind, her nose high. Just like on the range, for a split second our eyes met and a warm humming filled me. This was my horse, I just knew it, and her name came to me in the same instant. I decided I'd name her Prairie Rose—Rosie for short—because of the wild land she came from. That was a good name for a show jumper. I could see us flying over jump after jump at Spruce Meadows. First-place ribbons would be hung all over her stall.

"Okay. Let's find out whether she's numbered," Grandpa said, bringing me back to reality.

"Numbered?" I echoed.

"The horses should be numbered for the auction." Grandpa moved over toward a guy from the military base and asked him. The man looked at him blankly.

"You've got to be kidding," he said. "No one can get near these horses—it's been a flippin' rodeo. The fellows will let them in the corral one at a time and get the bidding started. If you've got one in mind, you'll have to pay attention."

Grandpa's face turned red. "There's twelve hundred horses here, man!" he sputtered.

"Yeah. This here auction could take a while, eh?" The man grinned.

Grandpa turned away in disgust. He looked at me, seemed on the verge of speaking, then stopped.

"Please, Grandpa?" I said beseechingly.

Grandpa reached out and ruffled my windblown hair. "We won't leave without her," he promised. "Let's go sign in and find a good place to watch."

Grandpa signed his name on a registration list and received a card with big black numbers.

"What's that for?" I asked.

"To hold up when you bid so the auctioneer can see you. When we get that mare, they'll write down my number. When I go to pay, they'll match the number to my registration," Grandpa explained. We were number twenty.

When the auction began, it began in earnest. The auctioneer—a fat man with greasy black hair and a broad, smiling face—had a voice so rich and rolling that his words flowed together like music. I almost had to stop myself from dancing to the rhythm, especially when two guys in black cowboy hats began pointing at the bidders and uttering short sharp yells at regular intervals. "Hargh!" or "Hup-hup!" they'd holler, pointing at the next bid in the crowd. At least, that's what it sounded like to me. Maybe it was actually a word in the English language, but I couldn't tell.

Everyone seemed to know what they were doing. Even Grandpa was following what was going on with interest. I had no clue, but all I could think of was Rosie. My feet itched and I couldn't keep my hands still. When would she be brought into the corral?

When she was, it took me by surprise. I'd been daydreaming about competing on Rosie when Grandpa nudged me in the ribs.

"This is it," he said.

"Now what a little beauty we have here!" shouted the auctioneer. "This little mare is around three years old, I'm told. Let's start the bidding at one-fifty. What-am-I-bid? One fifty, one fifty, one fifty..."

Grandpa lifted his card.

"I've got one fifty. One seventy-five. One seventy-five, anyone give me one seventy-five. One seventy-five in the corner. I've got one seventy-five. Two hundred, two hundred, who'll give me two hundred?" The auctioneer glanced at Grandpa. Grandpa nodded and lifted the card slightly again.

"Hup-hup!" yelled a man in a black cowboy hat, pointing out a new bidder to the auctioneer. The auctioneer's patter increased in speed until I could hardly make out any words. But the rhythm of the dance increased, and Grandpa was warring with two other bidders for my horse.

Three hundred. Then three fifty. I began to get worried. I only had four hundred and ten dollars.

Four hundred. One of the other bidders dropped out. Grandpa bid again.

Four twenty-five. I looked at Grandpa in despair. He smiled and bid one last time. Four fifty.

The auctioneer still prattled on, trying for five hundred. Grandpa wavered. The other bidder nodded and the auctioneer's gavel came crashing down.

"Sold to bidder number thirty-seven for five hundred dollars!"

chapter eight

I blinked back tears. I'd lost Rosie. Lost her! She was *mine*. My throat was so clogged I couldn't speak.

"I'm sorry, Reese." Grandpa squeezed my shoulder. "I didn't think the bidding would go so high for her."

"It's all right," I said thickly. "I only had four hundred and ten dollars. I didn't even have enough when you put in your last bid."

"I know. I was willing to help you out with the money. But I could've done a bit more, maybe."

"No, Grandpa. You've helped me a lot already. I don't want to take your money too." I knew that while Grandpa had enough, he sure didn't have a lot of extras. Most of what he earned went back into the ranch.

Grandpa nodded. "We could stay. Bid on another horse. There's certainly a lot to choose from."

I shook my head. "It wouldn't be the same. I wanted her and no other."

"I know," Grandpa said softly, and I knew he really did know. Horses were like friends, like people. They couldn't just be replaced. "We could find out who the new owners are and offer to buy her from them," he said.

"But we'd have to offer them more money," I objected. "And I don't have it."

"Well, it wouldn't hurt to see what they have to say. Maybe if they know you're interested, they'll change their minds. Especially if they get her home and have a tough time breaking her." Grandpa gave me a sly grin and I couldn't help but laugh, as dismal as I felt.

"All right," I agreed. I trailed after Grandpa, behind the corral, to a makeshift pen where the horses that had been sold were being roped and loaded into waiting trailers. The thought of driving the old truck back to the ranch with an empty trailer made my throat squeeze shut again.

Rosie was there. She whickered nervously at the sight of the cowboys with the rope. She tossed her head, but there was nowhere for her to run. I knew a halter would have been safer and more comfortable for her, but haltering an unbroken, fully grown horse was a tricky business. One of the men managed to slip the lasso over her head and tighten it around her neck. When she felt the rope, she fought fiercely, shaking her head and bracing her back feet.

"Whoa, there! Whoa!" yelled the cowboy.

My heart ached.

"Open the trailer door. I'll slacken the rope and see if she'll go in," the cowboy called to the trailer's owner.

When the trailer door was swung wide, Rosie spotted it as a possible escape route. The windows of the trailer made it appear open at the far side, so it didn't look like the dead end that it was. Rosie headed for it right away, and when she was safely inside, the owner swung the door shut.

Rosie's hooves made ringing thuds on the door as soon as she realized she was trapped, but that wasn't what startled me. It was the owner of the trailer.

It was Jim Bellamy.

chapter nine

"You are a giant pain in the butt," I said, a week after the auction, as I surveyed the mess Boots had just made. She'd been searching for carrots in my tack bag and managed to strew all of my riding kit over the stable floor, then step on it as well.

I began picking up my stuff and shoving it back in the bag. I was already dressed for my lesson, but I still needed my half-chaps, since I was wearing short boots, and now they had horse manure smeared all over them. "Nice," I told Boots.

She didn't care. She nipped at me, impatient for the carrots that she could smell but hadn't found.

"No way, sweetheart," I said sharply. "You'll get treats when you work for them and not before."

Boots laid back her ears at my tone. She danced sideways, clattering her hooves in warning on the concrete floor.

"Forget it. I'm not putting up with any of your attitude today," I told her. "So you'd just better behave or there'll be trouble. I've got enough to deal with without you."

That was the truth. I was still upset about losing Rosie. Funny, since she had never really been mine. I'd never even gotten the chance to get close to her, let alone touch her. But still, I felt as though I'd lost something important, something that I knew I had a lot of hopes for.

Grandpa had talked to Jim Bellamy, but I'd known it was no use. Bellamy wouldn't sell, and even if he did, he would want more money than I could afford. My mom and dad didn't want to give me any more—they'd already paid for riding lessons and all my tack, plus they had agreed to help pay for Rosie's feed and vet bills. I couldn't ask them for more.

I stepped into the stall to grab the saddle blanket that had fallen down when Boots had been nosing around. I stood up in a hurry when I heard Kayla's voice—angry and clipped.

"No way, Mom. That's totally unfair!"

There was a pause. I waited for someone to answer—presumably her mother—but there was no response. Then Kayla spoke again.

"But you and Dad never even made it to my last horse show! All you ever care about are your fancy friends and their stupid dinner parties," she whined.

Pause.

I finally figured out what was going on—Kayla was talking on her cell phone.

"I don't care!" Kayla shouted. "I'm not going, and you can't make me!" I heard the snap of the cell phone being closed and then Kayla stomped past Boots's stall. She didn't even notice me at first, but it was pretty obvious when she brought Twilight out and saw me standing there that I'd heard everything.

"Sorry," I said awkwardly.

Kayla looked away and began grooming Twilight. "It doesn't matter." She pressed her lips into a tight line.

"Are you okay?" I asked.

"Yeah," Kayla said. She leaned into the currycomb, making Twilight snort. She looked at me. "It's nothing."

"Sure. Right." I turned back to Boots and began to tack up. We worked in silence for a few minutes. Then Kayla spoke again.

"My mom wants me to skip my lesson on Saturday and go with them to visit some boring friends that my dad is trying to do business with," she said.

"You don't have to explain," I answered.

"I know, but it makes me so mad." Kayla threw her saddle on Twilight and cinched the girth. "There is no way I'm missing a lesson—especially for some dumb cocktail party. They just don't understand how important riding is to me."

"Looks to me like they understand plenty," I retorted. "You're acting like a spoiled little kid."

"What?" Kayla stared at me.

"Look at you! You have the best saddle, the fanciest tack, the nicest clothes and a fantastic horse. Seems like your parents must care a lot about your riding to spend that kind of money."

Kayla snorted. "That's what you think. Spending money means nothing to them. It's all about the show." She glanced at me sideways, her jaw hard. "And I *don't* mean horse shows."

"Huh?" I said.

"It looks good, their daughter being in show jumping, and it's something for them to brag about to their friends. But they couldn't care less about how I do when I compete with Twilight." Kayla frowned, her voice bitter.

She finished getting Twilight ready in silence. I really didn't know what to say. I always thought Kayla had everything–this was a bit of a shock.

"I still think you're spoiled," I muttered.

Kayla ignored me, took Twilight's reins and led him toward the arena. "See you in the ring," she said, without looking back.

chapter ten

Several weeks later, Kayla and I still weren't talking to each other. Our friendship wasn't exactly blooming. I strapped on my helmet, ready for another riding lesson, but my heart wasn't in it. Boots and I just didn't have it together, and I was beginning to believe that there wasn't much point in trying anymore.

"Hey, Reese," Laurel called, striding through the stable with a horse blanket over one arm. "Weren't you at that wild horse auction about a month ago?" She stopped beside Boots.

"Yeah. Why?" I slung the saddle over Boots's back and tightened the girth.

"There's an article about it in the newspaper." Laurel's face was grimmer than usual. "They're saying that some people are selling those horses for slaughter."

"*What!*" I shrieked. Boots pulled violently at her halter, startled at my voice. I caught her head and made soft shushing noises until she was quiet. "What are you talking about?" I asked Laurel in a whisper.

"It's a big scandal. Apparently some business guys—big ranchers or something—used other people's names to bid on the horses. How many were you allowed to buy?"

"I'm not sure. Three...five, maybe. Not very many."

"Well, some of these guys bought, like, fifty or more. And they've sold them to the slaughterhouses."

I felt sick, and Laurel looked about as bad as I felt. Anyone who loves horses doesn't like to see them hurt, but this was beyond horrible. To have those mustangs running free, then captured by men only to be slaughtered...I thought I might throw up.

"Did you get one?"

"One...what?" I said, my throat so constricted I could barely speak.

"A horse," Laurel said impatiently. "Did you get one of the wild horses?"

"No. No, I didn't," I answered.

"Why not?" Laurel eyed me curiously.

"The mare I wanted was sold to someone else," I said, my voice curt.

"Oh." Laurel bit her lip. "That's too bad. She's probably in good hands, though. I'm sure whoever bought her will take great care of her."

My hands went numb—I couldn't feel the halter, even though I was gripping it like a lifeline. Boots snorted warningly, but I didn't step back, didn't release her. I just stared at Laurel as blinding realization struck.

Jim Bellamy was not the kind of person who would take good care of Rosie. He was, however, exactly the kind of person who would sell her for meat if it made him enough money.

Now I really did feel sick.

"Are you okay?" Laurel asked. "You're white to the ears."

"Um...no. Could you untack Boots for me?" I asked. "I think I'm going to have to skip the lesson."

"Sure." Laurel looked concerned, but she took the lead rope and retied Boots to the post.

"Could I use your phone?" I said.

"Of course. It's in the office. The door's open." Laurel unbuckled the girth and slid the saddle off Boots's back.

I began to walk away. Then I thought of something and turned back. "Hey, Laurel?"

"Yeah?"

"How much money would someone get for horsemeat?"

Laurel paused, pursing her lips in thought. "Well, I'm no expert, but I think for a good-sized horse, anywhere from eight to around twelve hundred dollars."

Twelve hundred dollars! I swallowed.

"Thanks," I said. If Bellamy had purchased more horses, and he spent around five hundred a horse—which he didn't, I'm sure...my bidding had driven the price up on Rosie—he could make a profit of at least seven hundred dollars per horse. If he bought ten horses, that was seven thousand dollars!

I had to call Grandpa right away. If Bellamy had a chance to make that kind of money, he'd take it. I knew he would. And Rosie would end up—my head began to ache and I squeezed my eyes shut against the horrifying image that kept intruding. I would not let that happen to her. I had no idea what I was going to do yet, but I would think of something. I had to.

chapter eleven

The phone rang persistently, but no one answered. "Rats!" I slammed the receiver down and tried to think. How could I find out if Bellamy actually intended to slaughter those horses?

"Something wrong?" Kayla poked her head in the office door.

I closed my eyes. Kayla was absolutely the last person on earth I wanted to see right now.

"Reese?" Kayla persisted.

I opened my eyes. "Look, Kayla. No offense, but I've got some things going on right now and I really don't need you hassling me, okay?"

"Who's hassling you?" Kayla said. "I was looking for Laurel."

I took a deep breath and tried to marshal my thoughts. Think of Rosie. How can I save Rosie? "Sorry, Kayla, but I could use a little help."

"What?" Kayla blinked in confusion. "First you blast me and now you need my help? Reese, are you okay?"

"*Why* does everyone keep asking me that?" I yelled. "Yes, I'm okay. I'm fine. Everything's fine. I just need to *think* for a minute. Is that too much to ask?" I was ashamed to find tears leaking out of my eyes. I brushed them away impatiently, expecting Kayla to get mad, maybe stomp out of the office.

Instead she pulled over Laurel's extra chair, took off her helmet and sat down.

"What's wrong?" she asked. Her voice, if not exactly gentle, was at least sincere.

I gulped and then the whole story poured out. Kayla sat frozen when I finished.

"You think Bellamy will really..." She trailed off.

I nodded. "I'm sure of it. I just need to prove it. My grandpa will help, I know he will, but he's not home. So how am I supposed to get the proof?"

Kayla smiled wickedly. "That's easy."

"How?" I demanded.

"Phone the slaughterhouse."

"*What?*" I gripped the edge of the table.

"How many can there be?" Kayla spread her hands in an innocent gesture. "Phone information, get the number, call them, pretend to be Bellamy's secretary confirming the delivery or something and bingo! Either they tell you that there's no delivery scheduled or they tell you when it is. Easy."

My mouth was hanging open. "Are you kidding?"

"No. Don't be such a weenie. Haven't you ever made prank phone calls before?"

"Not since they invented call display," I said tartly, stung by the insult.

"Good point. Here, use my cell. The number won't come up." Kayla dug into her jacket pocket and handed me a sleek black phone.

"Thanks," I muttered. Then I glanced up. "Why are you doing this?" I asked point-blank. "We're not even friends."

"I know," Kayla answered matter-of-factly. "But I happen to love horses too, you know. If I can help you save this one, I will. That's all. It's not like I like you or anything."

"Oh. Good. Because I still don't like you either," I said.

Kayla raised one eyebrow. "The phone? Call information first."

I dialed 411. An operator's recorded voice came on. "For what city, please?" I panicked and hung up.

"What did you do that for?" Kayla demanded.

"They want to know what city. I have no idea," I said.

Kayla grunted in exasperation and reached for the yellow pages on Laurel's desk. "We'll try this first, then." But flipping through it gave us no leads. There was nothing under "slaughter."

"Try meat," I suggested. There were meat markets, meat wholesalers and meat packers. "Meat packers might be it," I said doubtfully.

"Yeah, but there's quite a few," Kayla answered. "Would Bellamy bring his horses into Calgary?"

"Maybe not. I tapped my chin thoughtfully with a pencil. "In fact, probably not. He's some kind of businessman in town. The ranch is kind of second for him. He probably wouldn't want the controversy if people found out. He'd take the horses somewhere else, some place harder to track."

"Okay, then. Let's phone information and get numbers for any place near Bellamy's ranch. I'll do the talking this time."

I didn't protest. I handed Kayla back her phone and waited while she dialed. She spoke to the operator like a pro and got the numbers of three different meat-packing companies. "I have no idea if these guys are slaughterhouses or what," Kayla said.

"But let's call and say we're calling on Jim Bellamy's behalf and ask if a delivery date has been set."

"Then what?" I asked.

"Then the secretary checks and either tells you yes or no." Kayla rolled her eyes. "Do you want me to call?" She tapped her fingernail impatiently against the phone.

"No. I'll do it." But my hands were trembling. The whole reason for this production had unnerved me. I reached for the phone and dialed.

Someone answered.

"Yeah?" It was a gruff, male voice.

This wasn't what I expected at all. I cleared my throat. "Is this Glenridge Packers?"

"Yeah." The voice was still a guttural croak.

"I...uh...am calling for Jim—James—Bellamy, to confirm a delivery date."

"Hang on, I'll check." The man dropped the phone with a clatter and there was a pause for several seconds. Soon he was back. "No Bellamy on the records. You sure you got the right place?"

"Maybe not. Thanks for checking." I hung up quickly and drew a deep breath.

"Well?" Kayla demanded.

"That's not it."

"Try the next one."

I was nervous, but Kayla pushed the phone back into my hands. I dialed again. This time I got a woman who answered more politely, which meant I had to lie more thoroughly. I was not a good liar.

"I'll have to look. What's the name again?" she said suspiciously.

I gave it to her and waited while I was put on hold. She came back on the line abruptly. "Mr. Bellamy is scheduled to deliver livestock this Friday."

"Oh. All right." I tried to sound official. "I'll let him know. Good-bye." I hung up and sank back in the chair.

"Well?" Kayla asked.

"They have Bellamy scheduled to deliver livestock tomorrow," I answered.

"What kind of livestock?"

"I don't know," I said irritably. "I thought it would be kind of obvious if I asked."

Kayla pursed her lips. "True. But now we have to find out. He could have cattle he's bringing in."

"What difference does it make?" I pointed out. "I know he's going there. Why can't I just sneak onto the ranch and let Rosie go?"

"Because if you do, you're going to be charged with theft!" Kayla snapped. "You have to prove that Bellamy is going to slaughter that horse, and then you can go to the guys who ran the auction and tell them that Bellamy is breaking the rules. Weren't those horses supposed to be kept for a least a year? They made that rule so people wouldn't turn around and make money off them."

"Yeah, but what if I can't get proof in time? What if the military guys won't listen to me? I'm a kid. What if they don't take me seriously?"

There were footsteps in the hall, and Laurel poked her head through the doorway before Kayla could answer. "The lesson started ten minutes ago, Kayla."

"Sorry." Kayla hastily put her helmet back on her head. "Don't worry," she whispered as she followed Laurel out. "We'll think of something."

chapter twelve

"I thought you'd understand," I said bitterly.

"I do understand. That doesn't mean I'd let you risk your neck, crawling around a pasture in the dark to let loose a bunch of wild broncs."

Grandpa had been in town to run an errand and stopped at my house for a coffee with my mom. When I finally gave up trying to phone him at the ranch, I called home to ask my dad to pick me up early from my riding lesson, and Grandpa answered the phone. When I told him what was going on, he came out right away and brought me back to the ranch for supper.

"Why not?" I cried.

"Because, Reese. It's dangerous. It's foolish. I'm not letting you go out there alone." Grandpa stood with his arms crossed in front of him.

I threw up my hands in frustration. "I will not sit back and let Jim Bellamy kill my horse!" I yelled. "If you think I'm not going to do anything–!"

"Whoa...hang on a second," Grandpa said calmly. "I said I wouldn't let you go out there *alone*. I'm coming with you."

"Well, of course you are," I answered crossly. "Who else is there to drive the truck?"

Grandpa stared at me, then started to chuckle. "You didn't let me in on that part of it."

"I wasn't sure you would do it," I said.

"I might not, except that I wouldn't put it past you to walk every step of the way if I didn't," Grandpa said.

I felt a grin twitch at the corners of my mouth. "I probably would," I admitted.

"But you need a plan," Grandpa continued.

"Well, I thought we could go out to the ranch when Bellamy isn't there, find some kind of proof that he's planning to ship the wild horses for meat and then show it to the auction officials."

"Mm-hmph." Grandpa stared at me with open skepticism. "And how will you do that, exactly? What kind of proof are you looking for? And how will you know when Jim will be out and when he'll be back so you'll have time to look for it?"

"I...don't know," I admitted.

Grandpa frowned. "It's a good thing you told me about this, because that plan is not going to work."

My shoulders sagged. I'd been so sure Grandpa would be able to offer some concrete help.

"Lucky for you, I know some things that you don't. If we think this through, we can probably pull it off."

"Really?" I shot him a hopeful glance.

"Slaughterhouses have to keep some fairly careful records," Grandpa explained. "After all the hoopla with mad cow disease, they have to be able to trace an animal back to its owner. Ranchers and farmers have to fill out forms on the animals they're bringing in. All we need to do is get those and it'll show that Jim Bellamy intends to slaughter the horses."

I heaved a sigh of relief. "That's great."

"Except there's a bit of a problem with that," Grandpa continued.

"What is it?" I said.

"Well, those forms have to be filled out when you're bringing the animals in. You can't do it ahead of time. I usually fill mine out the morning I'm shipping them in, and then they have to stay in the truck—that's a rule. The forms have to stay in the transport vehicle. So on the one hand, we know where they'll be, and we can watch for a chance to swipe them. But on the other hand, we only have a small window of opportunity to get the forms before Bellamy loads the animals. We want to get Rosie out of there, and once she's in the truck, we'll have a real fight on our hands."

"Are you saying we'll steal her?"

Grandpa shook his head. "No. But Bellamy could technically just drive away with her if she's in his truck. We need to get Rosie out of that corral and then take those forms to the auction officials. We should let them know ahead of time what we think Bellamy is up to."

"If we do that, can't they just take Rosie away from him?" I asked.

"Not unless we have proof that he is planning to slaughter her, and the only way to get it is to get our hands on those forms."

"Oh." I drew a breath. "Then I guess I'm staying here tonight. We'll have to get to Bellamy's ranch early."

"What about school?" Grandpa asked. "And your parents? I could deal with this without you—in fact, it would be safer for you if I did."

"But not safer for you. What if Bellamy catches you? No, I'm going," I said with determination. "Rosie's my horse, and I want to be there. I'll just have to talk to Mom and Dad."

chapter thirteen

I tugged on the door handle of Grandpa's truck in the gray early dawn. The door groaned on its rusty hinges, sounding obnoxiously loud in the morning stillness. I jumped in, glad to get out of the strong chinook wind blowing over the pasture.

I turned to look in the back for the toolkit—Grandpa figured we might need it—when the lumpy, wool blanket that was wadded up on the seat gave a sudden heave.

I stifled a yelp of surprise and pulled back, my heart hammering against my ribs. Could an animal have gotten in and nested in here last night? If so, it was pretty big and only inches away. I wondered if I could back slowly out of the truck, but as I reached behind me for the door handle, the lump of wool turned and heaved again, the blanket falling away.

I nearly fell off the seat. Kayla sat up and rubbed her bleary eyes. "Is it time to go yet?"

"What—" I gasped for breath, as much from relief that I wasn't about to get eaten as from shock that the last person I expected to be here suddenly was. "What are you doing here?"

"Helping, of course." Kayla covered her mouth with her hand. "Do you think there would be time for me to brush my teeth before we leave?"

I blinked. No, I definitely wasn't dreaming. She was still there. "Kayla, what's going on? How did you get here?"

"Same way you did—in your grandpa's truck. I hid back there when your grandpa picked you up from the stable last night." Kayla gestured to the narrow bench seat behind the front seats, where the toolkit, ropes and other stuff Grandpa kept back there usually sat.

I stared at her in disbelief. "You stowed away in the truck and slept here all night?"

Kayla shook her head. "Uh, mostly."

"You could have frozen to death! Or starved!" I yelled. "What were you thinking? And what about your mom and dad?"

"I phoned them and left a message that I was spending the night with a friend. My mom had a late meeting and my dad was out of town. I doubt very much they would have even noticed I was gone," she added bitterly. "And it wasn't very cold last night—if it was, I'd have come in the house. Now that you mention it, though, I *am* hungry."

I snorted in exasperation. "Come on." I shoved the door of the truck open and led Kayla toward the house. We met Grandpa on the back porch, wearing a wool hunting jacket and holding a steaming mug of coffee in one hand.

"Who's this?" he asked in puzzlement.

"This is Kayla Richards. She's...uh, a friend from riding lessons."

"Oh?" Grandpa waited to hear more.

"She spent the night in the truck."

"You did?" Grandpa glanced at her. When she nodded, he frowned. "Now why would you go and do a thing like that?" A flush of embarrassment colored Kayla's cheeks, but Grandpa went on. "That had to be mighty uncomfortable. You'd have been more than welcome in the house."

Kayla shifted her feet. "I wasn't sure," she muttered. "I didn't want you to send me home."

"She's hungry too," I put in.

"Well, of course she is," Grandpa said. "Come on, let's get you some breakfast." He opened the door to the house and led Kayla inside.

I showed her the bathroom, got her a fresh toothbrush and let her get cleaned up. Meanwhile, Grandpa was frying eggs. I put two thick slices of bread in the toaster.

"Fried egg sandwich and juice ought

to hold her," he said. "Grab a couple of bananas too, Reese." He deftly flipped the eggs onto the toast, clapped the second slice on top and put the whole thing into a plastic container. I stuffed two bananas and several juice boxes into a plastic grocery bag.

"Mmmm. Something smells great." Kayla walked into the kitchen. Her face had a fresh-scrubbed shine, and her hair was damp at the temples, but combed back. She looked a little out of place, though, in her riding breeches and knee-high boots, compared to Grandpa and me in our jeans.

"You can eat on the way," Grandpa told her. "We've got to get out to Bellamy's ranch before he loads up, and I don't know when that'll be. In fact..." Grandpa looked from Kayla to me. "Neither of you girls should be going. I can't take the responsibility for you, Reese, let alone Kayla. Do your parents know where you are?" He turned to Kayla suddenly.

"Sort of," Kayla said in a small voice. "I left them a message."

Grandpa smacked his forehead with

his palm. "What have I got myself into?" he asked.

"Grandpa, look at the time. We can't stand around arguing. Kayla came because she wanted to help rescue Rosie, and I'm not going to stay here at the ranch either. If you leave us here, I'll saddle up Paint and Old Ben and we'll ride across the fields to Bellamy's place. Or we'll take the tractor. Or hitchhike."

Grandpa's face twitched. I would never hitchhike anywhere, but I could see that last suggestion worried him. He sighed. "Come on, then. But you two will stay in the truck, understood?"

"Yes, sir," Kayla answered.

"Yes." I couldn't keep from smiling.

Grandpa handed Kayla the container with her sandwich. "Let's go."

chapter fourteen

The pre-dawn chill had intensified as heavy gray clouds thickened over the mountains to the west. The warm winds, which had made the temperature rise over the past few days, had shifted direction and turned icy cold.

"Feels like snow," Grandpa said, turning up the collar on his wool jacket. "Looks like the chinook is over."

"Good thing you weren't planning on sleeping in the truck tonight," I commented to Kayla. I shivered and turned up the heater.

We pulled off the main road onto a gravel drive that led to Bellamy's ranch. Grandpa parked the truck some distance from the house, partially hidden behind some pine trees, so the noise wouldn't alert anyone.

I followed him out of the truck.

"You get right back in there!" Grandpa said.

"But we can't see anything from here!" I protested. "How will I know you're okay?"

"Look, Reese, I'll hide near Bellamy's truck. When I see him leave the forms in there, I'll grab them and come straight back. Nothing to it."

"What about the dogs?" I asked. There were always dogs on a ranch. "If they bark..."

Grandpa patted his pocket. "I thought of that. I'm carrying ammunition."

Kayla stared. "What kind of ammunition?"

"Dog biscuits, of course." Grandpa grinned. "Now stay put. I'll be back."

Reluctantly, I climbed back in the truck. Kayla and I watched Grandpa disappear through the trees.

Kayla looked at me. "We're not really staying here, are we?"

"Not on your life," I answered. "Let's go." I jumped as the door creaked loudly, piercing the silence. I paused, but Grandpa did not reappear.

"Wait for me," Kayla whispered. She buttoned up her blazer and thrust her hands into her leather riding gloves.

"You sure you don't want your helmet?" I teased. She looked like she was ready to jump fences, not traipse through the bushes.

"I'm cold, and I didn't really plan this out, okay?" Kayla retorted. "You're not exactly a fashion plate yourself."

That was true. I hadn't stopped at home for clothes, so I was wearing one of Grandpa's old flannel shirts, which came down nearly to my knees, my jeans and jacket, his woolen tam, and mismatched gloves—one navy wool, the other black leather.

"No one's looking at us anyway," I said. "Let's get going."

We stepped carefully through the trees, trying to be as quiet as possible, following the direction Grandpa had taken. The pine boughs lifted and swayed in the wind; the ground was crusty with remnants of ice. It seemed like we'd been walking for hours when Kayla pushed aside a clinging branch and we reached the edge of a pasture. I could see a house at the far end, painted white with river-stone pillars along the porch—nice. Probably expensive too. There were several outbuildings—a shed, a large barn, a garage. I could also see a corral, and there were quite a few horses in it.

"Let's get closer." Kayla nudged me.

I didn't need to be told twice. We skirted the edge of the pasture, creeping toward the corral. A big semitrailer was parked nearby. I couldn't see Grandpa anywhere.

Kayla nudged me again, tilting her head toward the semi. I gave a quick nod, and we slunk through the bushes, trying not to be visible from the house.

I *did* hear a dog barking and winced as it became louder. Bellamy was sure to come out of the house if it didn't stop soon. The dog burst out of the trees, snuffing eagerly at the ground. Something came flying out of the bushes, and the dog leaped for it, crunching it between its teeth.

"What was that?" Kayla said.

I stifled a giggle. "Grandpa's throwing the dog treats." The dog looked up and waited, wagging its tail. Another dog biscuit sailed out. The dog gulped it down, then circled the bushes, but it didn't bark.

I breathed a sigh of relief. There was no sign of anyone near the house or the barn. If ever Grandpa was going to get those forms, now was the time...

I saw him slide out of the bush and edge toward the passenger side of the semi. He gingerly tried the handle. It opened easily, and Grandpa stepped up to look inside.

The next few seconds seemed to last for hours, but at last I saw Grandpa emerge with a fistful of papers in one hand. At the same time I heard the crunch of gravel. Jim Bellamy appeared suddenly in the doorway of the barn, leading a horse by its halter, in full view of the truck. I had no time to warn Grandpa. Bellamy looked startled, like someone who's walked into a room full of people with green hair, but he soon recovered.

He tethered the horse and strode over to the semi. "Hey, Gus. Something I can help you with?"

Grandpa's expression was bland, giving nothing away. "Maybe. I've been told you're shipping some horses today."

"Yeah. So?" Bellamy said.

"So, I have reason to believe that at least one of them is a wild horse from the military auction," Grandpa answered.

"And what difference would that make?" Bellamy said.

"The rules were pretty clear about not selling those horses for meat," Grandpa retorted. He waved his handful of forms.

Bellamy stopped, his eyes narrowing. "I could have you arrested for breaking and entering, Gus, not to mention theft if you intend to go anywhere with those manifests."

"Good!" Grandpa bristled. "Go ahead. We'll see what the police have to say when they have a look at those forms."

Bellamy grinned, a cold grin that sent shivers down my spine. "They won't say anything. They can't prove a thing. Those horses were slicks."

That halted Grandpa in his tracks.

"There's nothing on them to say that they weren't mine in the first place. How are you going to prove that the horses I'm shipping are the ones I bought at the auction?" Bellamy continued.

"What are slicks?" Kayla whispered.

"Horses that aren't branded." I felt my stomach clench. Bellamy was right—unless the military had kept exact records of who bought what horse, or had branded them all, there was no way to differentiate between Bellamy's horses and the wild horses. They'd all have Bellamy's brand now.

"You low-down slimy skunk," Grandpa sputtered.

"Hand over the forms, Gus," Bellamy said with an air of menacing patience. "I'm not about to lose a forty-thousand-dollar profit to an old man who wants me to play by the book."

"How many of those horses did you buy?" Grandpa asked, astonished.

"Some fifty head." Bellamy tipped back his hat.

"How...?" Grandpa said.

"Other people's names on the registration. Some were legitimate. My mother, for instance, God rest her soul. Others, not so much. Fred Flintstone made it on there I think. The auction officials didn't seem to notice."

Grandpa stared at him in utter disbelief. "You planned this all along. My granddaughter wanted that mare, and you bid against her. And all along you knew you were planning to destroy them."

Bellamy shrugged. "Your granddaughter can buy another horse. Didn't I tell her the only good reason for owning a horse was to make money, and jumping over fences didn't pay? There's good money to be made on these broncs, and I don't aim to let anyone stand in my way."

The implied threat was there. But Grandpa didn't budge. "Is that so?" he said evenly before he hauled off and punched Bellamy right in the gut.

"Grandpa!" I gave a small shriek.

"Ooof," Bellamy grunted, leaning forward and clutching his stomach. He straightened immediately, reached for Grandpa's jacket and shoved him up against the truck. Grandpa tried to push back, but with the forms in one hand he couldn't get Bellamy off. Bellamy had his hands around Grandpa's throat.

"The forms, Gus," Bellamy said through gritted teeth. Grandpa's face turned a deep brick red and he struggled for breath. Bellamy squeezed harder. I couldn't stand it any longer.

I sprinted out of the bushes and charged like a rampaging bull, leaping onto Bellamy's back. "Let him go!" I said fiercely, pounding the man's shoulders with one fist. Bellamy shrugged off the blows, hardly noticing them, still keeping his hands around Grandpa's throat.

I saw Grandpa's eyes begin to roll back in his head, and in a fit of desperation I wound up and slapped Bellamy with an open palm as hard as I could over the hollow of his ear.

He reacted then, whirling around to shake me off. My shoulder smacked into the bottom of the open truck door, sending a sharp spasm of pain down my arm. It was enough to loosen my hold, and I fell off into the dirt.

But I had accomplished what I set out to do. Bellamy had let go of Grandpa when I hit him. Grandpa's face lost that purplish look, and he drew great gulping breaths of air. I scrambled to my feet, ignoring the ache in my arm, and rushed to his side.

"Are you okay?" I asked.

He nodded grimly. He still had the forms in his fist and he thrust them at me. "Run," he whispered. "I'll take care of him." He nodded toward Bellamy, who was shaking his head, as though to dispel the ringing in his ears, but was also advancing on us.

I wasn't too sure about leaving Grandpa, but he shoved me away as Bellamy lunged for the papers in my hand. He ripped them away from me just as Grandpa stuck out a foot, tripped Bellamy and sent him sprawling. "Run!" Grandpa bellowed at me, his fists bunched, ready for Bellamy's next attack.

I had no choice. I ran.

I dove into the bushes, where Kayla was still huddled. "Come on!" she urged, grabbing my sleeve. She tugged me through the trees at a dead run.

"We...need...to call...for help," I gasped.

"I know!" Kayla cried. "What do you think I've been doing in those bushes, knitting? My cell phone isn't getting a signal. We need to get to higher ground."

I felt a surge of relief. I'd forgotten about Kayla's cell phone. If Grandpa could just hold Bellamy off long enough for help to come...

We dashed past the barn and corral, up a rocky incline.

"Keep running!" Kayla panted.

"Check the signal," I said.

She flipped the phone open as we climbed and shook her head. "Not yet." My breath caught in my side and my arm throbbed, but I ran harder, pulling Kayla with me. My leg muscles burned in protest as we reached the crest. "Try again," I wheezed, bending double, pressing my hand into the cramp under my ribs. If we didn't get a signal here, I didn't know what we'd do. This was the highest point on the ranch.

Kayla hit the power button and was rewarded with a faint metallic beep. "Bingo!" she cried in triumph.

"Call nine-one-one," I said. "Get the police, tell them it's an emergency, then meet me back at the barn."

Kayla was already dialing. She nodded and gave me a thumbs-up sign, then smacked the phone in frustration. "Darn it! It cut out!"

"Try again!" I cried.

I bounded back down the hill, taking care not to trip over rocks. Now that help was on the way for Grandpa, I had one thing I needed to do. I reached the corral a lot more quickly than I expected and searched for the gate that opened into the pasture. Bellamy's ranch was big, and even though the land was fenced, it would take him a lot longer to load those horses if they weren't in the corral.

I spotted the gate at the far end and

sprinted for it. It was chained, but fortunately not locked. As I wrestled with the chain, trying to undo the twisted knot it had been tied in, I saw Rosie among the other horses. She stood out, her bright chestnut coat a spot of red among the browns and grays. She came closer to the fence. I wouldn't have expected her to come anywhere near me, but maybe she thought I had food, or maybe she anticipated escape. In any case, I got the chance to watch her for a moment, and I felt my heart contract.

"Not today," I told her in a whisper. "Whether you're with me or running wild out there, I will not let him hurt you." And I yanked the chain free.

chapter fifteen

The racket from the chain startled Rosie. I swung the gate wide. The big mare hesitated, and in that split second I saw something on her flank–a rough, C-shaped arch, an old brand of some kind. It was small, with a blurred smudge of letters underneath, and the hair had grown into it, making it almost invisible. I got behind her and flapped my arms at her. "Go on!" I shouted. "Get going!"

She shied, then bolted through the open gate, running out into the meadow. The rest of the horses, their ears pricked, followed at a gallop. Within seconds the corral was empty.

I sprinted back toward the barn, fear for Grandpa sending a burst of adrenaline through me. As I rounded the back of the building, I spotted an object on the ground. I bent to pick it up, panic rising in my throat. It was Kayla's cell phone. I slipped it in my jacket pocket and listened hard, but there was no sound except for the gentle whickering of the horse Bellamy had led out earlier, still tethered to the fence.

Where was Kayla? She had obviously been here. And where was Grandpa? I peeked around the corner of the barn, but there was no sign of anyone. Even Bellamy's truck was gone.

I sank to the ground, my mind spinning with possibilities. Had Grandpa and Kayla made a run for the truck? I didn't think so. Grandpa wouldn't leave me stranded unless he absolutely had to. And what about

Bellamy? It wasn't likely that he'd popped out for groceries, not in that big rig. So why would he take a huge truck, that would hold dozens of horses, if it wasn't loaded?

I just didn't get it.

A red pickup truck pulled up the long drive from the main road and parked near the house. I flattened myself against the barn wall, behind some hay bales and a stacked assortment of rusty old tools.

A man got out, glanced around the yard, then strode up to the house. He was about thirty and had the ruddy look of someone who spent most of his time outdoors. There was no answer to the doorbell, so he ambled back after a moment, frowning. Then he sighed and reached inside the red pickup for a thermos cup. He leaned against the bumper of the truck and sipped the steaming liquid from the cup.

I was trapped.

I couldn't move from my hiding spot with that guy there, couldn't look for Grandpa or Kayla, even if I knew where to look. The minutes ticked past. The man looked at his watch. I struggled with the idea of making a run for it, but the heavy vibration of an engine interrupted my worried thoughts. I glanced up to see Bellamy's truck toiling up the drive from the opposite end. Bellamy cut the engine of the semi just in front of the barn.

The guy walked over from the pickup just as I heard the semi's door slam.

"Hey, Jim," the man said, "ready to load 'em up?"

"Yeah," Bellamy said gruffly. "Sorry I'm late. I had a problem with the truck. Had to take it down to the shed and grab a few tools."

The younger man looked interested. "What was wrong?"

"Nothing," Bellamy snapped. "Just a few bolts loose on the trailer. The door was rattling."

The younger man scratched his head. "That doesn't sound like much of a problem," he commented. He looked puzzled—and so was I. Why would Bellamy waste time fixing loose bolts when he obviously had more pressing things to deal with? If Grandpa and Kayla had gotten away with the forms, Bellamy would be trying to stop them, and if they hadn't, then they should still be here. I tried to suppress a jolt of fear. Something was definitely wrong.

Bellamy ignored the man. "I'll back the trailer up to the gate. The horses managed to get out of the corral, but if you saddle Hoser and take the dogs, you should be able to get them in pretty quick."

The younger man snorted. "You call your horse *Hoser*?"

"Yeah, it's from that old SCTV skit. And trust me, he is a hoser. Totally brainless. Once you help me load up, you can go."

"I thought you wanted me to start working some of your colts today," the younger man said.

"Not anymore," Bellamy answered quickly. "I'll still pay you for the day, though."

The younger man shrugged. "Okay. Whatever. Let's get started." I heard him go inside the barn. There was a scraping noise right above me as a saddle was lifted off the wall. I sank back, mentally ticking off all the clues.

Grandpa and Kayla had disappeared.

Bellamy was still going ahead with his plan to ship the horses.

He had taken the truck and gone somewhere—maybe to the shed, as he claimed. But what was he doing there? Loose bolts shouldn't be much of a problem—anyone with a wrench could take care of that. Why a special trip to the shed?

And then the pieces came together.

What if Bellamy had managed to lock Grandpa in the horse trailer? It would have been no big deal for Bellamy to force Kayla in there too.

I didn't think Bellamy would really hurt them. He could get serious jail time for that, and Bellamy was in this to make a fast buck. He just needed them out of the way long enough so he could carry out his plans. He probably drove them somewhere in the trailer, tied or locked them up, then came back to load the horses. It couldn't be far away either, or else he wouldn't have gotten back so fast.

I peeked between the hay bales, my gaze landing on the log shed Bellamy had stopped at in the truck. It was at the end of the drive, nearly at the road, half visible through the bushes.

The shed. It seemed too obvious. But, after all, there weren't many other choices. And it did make sense—Bellamy didn't really need to take the truck all the way down there to tighten a few bolts with a wrench. That was just a flimsy excuse to avoid having the hired guy ask too many questions.

By the time Grandpa and Kayla managed to get free—if they could—it would be too late. I swallowed hard at that thought. Bellamy would have his money and it would be our word against his that it had been the wild mustangs that were slaughtered.

I shuddered and clasped my hands tightly to stop them from shaking. Bellamy backed the truck up to the corral gate, and the younger man stepped out from the barn and saddled Hoser. I crouched even lower to the ground as he swung up into the saddle. Bellamy whistled for the dogs, which set off with the younger guy and the horse right away. Bellamy busied himself setting up the ramp into the trailer, then walked into the corral, out of my line of sight.

My stomach was so knotted with worry that I felt sick. What if Grandpa had a heart attack or something? I couldn't just sit here. I needed to investigate that shed. Bellamy was on the other side of the barn. I'd never have a better chance.

I took off running, dodging as silently as possible behind the bushes and bracken that edged the drive. Once I was hidden, I stopped running, creeping instead. I knew that every branch and twig snapped like a gunshot, and if I moved fast the swaying of the bushes would be a dead giveaway that someone— me!—was there.

My heart gave great leaping thuds and I gasped for breath as hard as if I'd run a mile uphill. Calm down, I told myself. Bellamy hasn't seen you. But I knew he would be watching for me.

The log shed was about five hundred meters away, but when you go that distance on your hands and knees, it seems a lot longer. When I finally gave a careful glance around and emerged from the bushes, I felt like I'd been crawling through them for more than an hour. Lucky for me, the door to the shed was on the opposite side from the barn, so neither Bellamy nor the other guy could see me from the barn.

"Grandpa?" My voice was hoarse. I put my mouth right up next to the door. "Kayla? Are you in there?"

chapter sixteen

The shed was silent and I felt my heart sink.

Then I heard a soft shuffling noise. Grandpa's whisper was only a croak. "Reese?"

"Grandpa!" I stifled the urge to shout with joy. "Are you and Kayla all right?"

"Well, I've had better days," Grandpa said. "And Kayla's pretty shook up. But we're okay."

"Can you get us out, Reese?" Kayla's voice sounded thin and scared.

I looked at the door. It was bolted with a heavy cast-iron latch, and there was a padlock threaded through the casings. "It's locked," I said.

"Can you break it?" Grandpa asked.

"Not without tools. A saw or something," I answered. "If I had a screwdriver, I could take it apart."

"There are a lot of screwdrivers in here," Grandpa said. "But that doesn't help."

"I'll look and see if I can find something." I searched around the perimeter of the building, but there was nothing except a rusty rake leaning against the woodpile, and an old tire.

"I'll have to go back up to the barn," I said through the door.

"You can't!" Kayla sounded panicky. "Bellamy will catch you for sure."

"Well, what am I supposed to do?" I demanded. "This door is solid wood. I can't break it down."

"Karate-chop it," suggested Kayla.

"I'd break my wrist," I said, but Kayla had given me an idea.

Chop it. I looked over at the woodpile. I hadn't really searched in there, but where there is split firewood, there should be an axe. I investigated, and, sure enough, an axe—rusty and weathered, but still sharp—was buried in a thick stump.

I wrenched it free with a few wiggles and a mighty tug. "Stand back," I said. I swung the axe as hard as I could at the door. It bit into the wood with a jarring thunk and stuck there.

"Well, that didn't work," I muttered. The heavy door remained fully intact, without even a crack. I yanked at the axe, but it wouldn't budge. I had to work it loose bit by bit.

"Try chopping at the wood around the latch," Grandpa said from behind the door. "Maybe you can knock one side loose."

I heaved the axe up and let it fall. The axe glanced off the metal with a ringing clang. I hoped the horses were making enough noise that Bellamy wouldn't notice the racket I was making.

"Try again. Aim for the wood just above the casing," Grandpa said.

I did. I tried , but I finally stopped, my arms aching. Only a few slivers had flaked off the door. "It's no use," I panted. "I can't do it."

I peered around the corner of the shed. I could see Bellamy beginning to load the horses. The younger man helping him had tethered Hoser and was ushering Rosie up the ramp. They must have managed to recapture all the horses.

"Grandpa, are you guys okay in there?" I asked, sliding back to the shed's door.

"It's not exactly a four-star hotel, but we're fine. Why?" Grandpa said.

"Bellamy's loading the horses and he's got Rosie." I steadied my voice. "I've got to find a way to stall him until the police come."

"I don't know if the police are coming!" Kayla cried. "The signal kept cutting out when I was talking. And then I lost the phone when Bellamy grabbed me."

"It's okay. I found it," I said. "I'll keep trying to get a signal. But I can't let Bellamy just drive away with the horses."

"Don't, Reese. Please. Bellamy really means business. He's not going to let you get in his way." Grandpa sounded worried.

"I won't. I'll just let the air out of his tires or something. I'll be right back." I dove into the bushes and began to weave through the bracken in a crouching run. I slowed down as I approached the barn. I wasn't as worried about being seen—Bellamy had his hands full with loading up the wild mustangs. They were scared and fighting. Rosie gave a shrill whinny as the younger cowboy prodded her with a long stick. Bellamy cracked a whip behind her and she bolted forward, right up the ramp into the trailer. I couldn't get near the truck tires without being spotted.

"Hey-yup!" Bellamy shouted, cracking the whip again. The younger man guided the last of the horses through the gate and into the trailer, then shut the trailer doors with a clang and dropped the latch in place.

"That takes care of it, boss," he said.

"Good." Bellamy took off his hat and wiped his forehead. "You can take off now. I'll drive them straight in."

"Okay. Give me a call when you want to start breaking the colts." The younger man strode to his pickup and got in. The engine roared to life. He let in the clutch and bumped carefully over the rutted drive, around the pasture and out to the main road.

I realized with sick certainty that I'd missed my chance. I could hardly have vandalized the truck with the two men standing there, but the younger cowboy might have helped me stop Bellamy if he knew my story. Now I was alone.

Bellamy opened the door to the semi's cab, ignoring the squeals and thuds that were coming from the trailer. He turned the ignition and carefully pulled the semi forward, the trailer rocking and heaving on the uneven road.

The horses inside were terrified. The sharp bang of hooves on metal made me catch my breath. Bellamy's horse, still tethered to a fencepost, yanked at his bridle and whinnied in reply. As the truck wound its way down the U-shaped drive, I looked over at Bellamy's horse. I had an idea.

The semi had driven into a copse of trees, so I snuck out of my hiding place. "Hi, Hoser, old boy," I said in a wheedling voice, approaching the horse. "Nice, Hoser." He laid back his ears—never a good sign. "It's all right, Hoser. Nobody's going to hurt you. I just want to take you for a little ride. Won't that be fun?"

I kept talking to him as I reached into my pocket and pulled out a limp carrot. It had been in there since yesterday, when I was going to have my riding lesson, but I figured Hoser wouldn't know the difference. His ears came up and I let him smell the carrot. Come on, come on, I thought impatiently. As slow as he was going, Bellamy was getting farther and farther down the road. I didn't have much time.

Hoser crunched the carrot thoughtfully and nosed me, looking for more. "Sorry, pal," I told him. "No more." I untied the reins, put one foot into the stirrup and swung up. It was a Western saddle, so it felt a little weird, but I settled into my seat, held the reins with firm hands and gave Hoser a squeeze with my legs.

He didn't budge.

"All right, then," I muttered. "I can see you're called Hoser for a reason." I delivered a sharp kick to his ribs. I didn't have spurs, but it seemed to do the trick. Hoser bolted forward and began to canter. I gripped him with my knees and steered him toward the pasture. Bellamy had to take the long, U-shaped drive to the road, but Hoser and I could cut him off if we went straight across the pasture.

Bellamy would never be able to turn that big truck and trailer around on this narrow, bumpy drive, so he had to be driving forward—slowly, too, or he'd bottom out on the ruts. He'd pass right by Grandpa's truck. The keys were still in it. If I could pull it across the road before Bellamy got there, he'd be stuck. If I could get the cell phone to work, then the police would be on their way. If I could convince them of what Bellamy was up to, convince them to get those forms...

Hoser clearly didn't want me on his back, but I clung to him, trying to get the rhythm of his rough gallop. The barbed wire fence was just ahead. With a quick prayer, I gave Hoser the signal to jump and hoped like anything that someone had taught him what to do. My heart was in my throat as Hoser leaped.

We sailed over the fence, landing with an ungraceful thump on the other side. Hoser's hind legs slipped on the ice-crusted mud, and for a minute I thought we'd go down. Instead he scrambled up and immediately took off through the trees. I had to duck to keep from being lashed across the face by branches.

I slowed Hoser and guided him through the woods so we could come out near Grandpa's truck. "We're almost there," I told him.

I could hear Bellamy's truck shifting gears through the trees. I slid out of the saddle and tied Hoser a good distance away.

"Good boy," I said, giving him a heartfelt pat on the neck. Then I yanked on the door of Grandpa's truck and dove inside. I fumbled with the keys, my hands shaking. I jammed my foot down on the clutch.

I didn't really know how to drive. Grandpa had let me drive the tractor before, but that was it. The ignition turned over and the engine coughed and sputtered to life. I gently let the parking brake in and hit the gas. The engine roared, but I didn't go anywhere.

My palms were slick with sweat. I let the clutch out and gave it less gas. The engine gave an abrupt thrum, the truck lurched forward a few inches, and the engine died.

"Oh, no!" I turned the key, but this time the old truck refused to budge.

chapter seventeen

Rrr-Rrr-Rrr, went the engine.

I closed my eyes. "Not now," I said. I turned the key again, but nothing happened. Bellamy's truck sounded louder—it was getting close. Grandpa's truck was too heavy for me to push it out into the drive, especially without help. I checked Kayla's cell phone and dialed 911, but there was still no signal. I tucked it inside my shirt pocket and shook my head in desperation. I'd tried so hard, and now to fail, like this. Bellamy was going to drive right past me with Rosie in that trailer, and there wasn't a single thing I could do about it. Tears stung my eyes, and a solid lump in my throat stopped me from swallowing. I wanted to bawl, but I blinked hard, willing myself not to cry.

"There has to be another way," I said. I got out of the truck. I could see Bellamy's trailer through the trees. He would be here in a matter of moments. I looked wildly around for something else that could block the road—rocks, a fallen log, anything. But the only things around me were poplar saplings, sparse fir trees, trampled grasses and fresh cow pies. Bellamy must let his cattle pasture through here, I thought. It was funny to notice such an ordinary detail when I had a crisis to deal with, but there they were—big ones that were still wet, not dried or frozen solid.

I picked up a cow pie in my—lucky for me—gloved hands. "Eeeuuuw!" I wrinkled my nose. "This is totally disgusting!" I told Hoser. "But it's my last chance." I armed myself with

several heaps of cow manure and ducked behind a fir tree.

Bellamy's truck bumped over the road. He'd picked up a little speed, knowing that the main road wasn't much farther. There was a faint noise coming from the cell phone in my pocket, but with my hands full of wet manure I couldn't do anything about it.

I watched the truck come closer...

"Now!" I yelled, flinging the cow pie at the windshield. It hit square in the center, splattering in a wide circle. My next shot hit the hood, but it sprayed upward, adding to the general mess.

The truck lurched to a stop. Bellamy swore and jumped out of the truck. "What do you think you're doing!" he yelled. In two strides he was in front of me, his face contorted with rage.

"You keep away from me, you filthy liar, or you'll get a faceful of this stuff next," I told him, backing quickly away. I held up a third handful of manure.

Bellamy's lips twitched. "Honey, I shovel this stuff every day. You think I'm not used to it by now?" He advanced slowly. "Now you listen to me. You and your grandpa are going to keep your mouths shut about those horses, understand me? Or there'll be trouble. Big trouble."

"What are you gonna do? Lock me up in the shed, like you did to my grandfather and my friend Kayla?" I countered, my knees quivering with fear. I was careful to speak very loudly and clearly. "That's kidnapping, in case you didn't know, Jim Bellamy. You can't threaten me. I'll tell whoever I want about this, and you can't stop me."

"Oh, can't I? Your grandpa's having a hard time scraping money together to keep that ranch running, isn't he? How would it be if things got just a little bit harder? You wouldn't want ol' Granddad to lose the farm, now would you?"

"You couldn't do that," I whispered, forgetting to talk loudly.

"Try me," Bellamy said, his eyes glittering like a snake's.

"All right, I will," I said defiantly. I'd heard another faint noise from my pocket, and it bolstered my courage. I sure hoped my hunch was right. I launched my final handful of cow manure straight at Bellamy, dodged behind a tree and dove into the open door of the semi's cab. The livestock manifests were sitting right on the passenger seat of the truck. Obviously Bellamy had thought he was home free.

I stripped off my dirty gloves and grabbed the forms, listening to Bellamy swear viciously as he wiped filth off his face with one sleeve. I'd gone way past being frightened. I was numb with terror as the man strode to the truck and stood in front of the driver's door, his face livid.

"You little..." He swore again. "I've had enough of these games. Give me those forms, little girl."

One of the horses whinnied from the trailer. "No," I said.

"Don't make me come in there after you," said Bellamy.

I didn't move.

Bellamy climbed into the truck. Instantly I opened the passenger door and flew out. And, at last, the sound I'd been waiting for finally reached my ears. The wail of a police siren was cut off as a cruiser pulled into Bellamy's drive.

One of the officers got out of the car, one hand on his holster. "Mr. Bellamy?" he asked. He wrinkled his nose at the smell coming from the windshield of the truck and the front of Bellamy's shirt.

"Yes." Bellamy stepped out of the truck and shot me a warning glance.

"We've been called to an assault complaint at this residence. Would you be willing to answer a few questions?" The second officer got out of the car.

"Absolutely." Jim Bellamy drew himself up and put on an oily smile. "I believe it was mostly a misunderstanding by my neighbor. His granddaughter here can explain."

Bellamy glanced at me, his eyes full of vicious meaning. A picture of Rosie, running free, crossed my mind. Then the thought of Grandpa losing his farm overshadowed it. I opened my mouth, but for a moment I didn't know what to say. I still hadn't been able to check my hunch about that cell phone.

"Yes." I heard my voice crack. "Everything's..." I paused as a horse whinnied again from the trailer. I was sure it was Rosie. I took a fresh grip on my courage. "...definitely not a misunderstanding," I answered firmly. Bellamy stared at me in disbelief as I brandished the livestock manifest forms in one hand. "Mr. Bellamy has filled out these forms, showing that he is shipping a bunch of horses to a slaughterhouse today. Those horses were bought at a military auction of wild mustangs, and the rules of that auction said that those horses were not to be sold for meat.

"But my friend Kayla called you today because when we tried to confront Mr. Bellamy about this, he punched my grandfather and locked him and Kayla in a shed up the road. And now he just told me that if I didn't keep my mouth shut about the wild horses, he would make sure my grandpa loses his ranch."

"Can you prove any of those allegations, young lady?" the officer said.

"Yes." I handed the officer the manifests while Bellamy glowered at me.

"Do you have anything to add?" The officer addressed Bellamy.

"Yes. First of all, Gus Drayton, who is the girl's grandfather, assaulted me first. It was simple self-defense on my part."

With a sinking feeling, I remembered that Grandpa *did* hit him first.

"When I finally got the man off me, I attempted to leave the premises before anything else could happen. He refused to let me leave with my livestock shipment, and I was forced to incarcerate the man in my shed, just so I could get off my own property. Then I found myself assaulted a second time, this time with cow manure on my truck." Bellamy waved an arm in an outraged gesture toward his windshield.

The officer's nostrils twitched. I pulled the cell phone out of my pocket and glanced at it to confirm that it was still connected.

"What about how you threatened to force my grandfather off his ranch?" I demanded.

Bellamy faced me with a bland expression. "I don't know what you think you heard, young lady, but you must have been imagining things."

"Oh, I don't think so." My smile didn't waver. I held up the cell phone in triumph. "Funny thing about cell phones. Sometimes you get a signal, sometimes you don't. The nine-one-one dispatcher just heard the whole thing."

chapter eighteen

Bellamy's face lost a little color, but he kept his composure. The officer began leafing through the manifests. I edged closer to him so I could get a look at them too.

"We can confirm that story with the dispatcher, sir," the officer said. "Maybe you'd better tell me what's going on."

"Officer, you have to understand my position. I've done nothing wrong here. The horses I am shipping are my horses. They are branded with my ranch's brand. I'm a well-known businessman as well as a rancher, and you can imagine the outcry if this girl spread rumors that I've sold wild horses for meat. It could damage my reputation with my clients. I'm not interested in making trouble, but I did tell the girl to keep quiet about the horses. If I've scared her, I'm sorry, but I can't let my business interests fall prey to a little girl who thinks she has a cause on her hands."

I felt a wave of frustration wash through me. That man had an answer for everything! I could see the police officer nodding as he read through the manifest. Everything Bellamy said made sense, and I had nothing to prove otherwise. I gritted my teeth at this helplessness. If Grandpa were here, he could help, but by the time the officer questioned him, the policeman would already have made up his mind which one of us he believed.

But then I saw, as the officer paused to read the manifests, a heading for "Other Brands" on the form. Written below it were the words "C-shaped crescent" letters "M" and "E." I drew in my breath. That was the brand—the old brand—on Rosie. It was the one identifying mark, which Bellamy *had* to report on the manifest, that would show she was one of the wild mustangs.

I could barely contain the grin of relief that spread over my face. Bellamy was watching me, and his expansive smile shrank to a small thin line. He knew something was up.

"Well, that about takes care of everything," the officer began, but I cleared my throat.

"Officer?" I said. "I think you'll find something on that form that will prove everything I've been saying." I pointed to the section for brands. "That brand is on the mare I bid for at the military auction. She's a red chestnut with one white sock. She's in the back of the trailer right now. This proves Mr. Bellamy planned to sell her for meat, in spite of the auction rules. That's fraud."

"What about this girl willfully damaging my property?" Bellamy countered. He gestured to his filthy truck.

The officer's lips twitched. "Well, I've never had to write up a report with cow manure listed as the weapon, but I guess there's always a first time."

"Look, what I do with an animal after I buy it should be my business," Bellamy said hotly.

"Not if you sign an agreement like the auction registration that says you have to keep the horse for at least a year!" I retorted. "And signing a false name, like Fred Flintstone, would be fraud too!"

The officer lifted one eyebrow. "Fred Flintstone?"

"I heard him talking to my grandpa," I said. "He admitted to buying at least fifty of the wild horses and signing other people's names. Fred Flintstone was one of them."

The officer nodded. "Yep, that would be fraud, all right. Sir, I'll have to ask you to come with me."

"No! I've done nothing wrong, I'm telling you. You'd take the word of a teenage girl over a reputable businessman like myself? This is ridiculous. I want to talk to a lawyer," Bellamy sputtered.

"Oh, you'll have that chance," the officer assured him. He snapped the handcuffs on

Bellamy's wrists and guided him into the backseat of the police car.

"This is unbelievable! What gives you the right to handcuff me?" I could still hear Bellamy blustering as the police officer slammed the door shut, cutting off Bellamy's voice.

The officer rubbed his forehead and sighed. "Where did you last see your grandfather?" he asked me.

"He's locked in a log shed at the other end of the drive, near the main road. My friend Kayla is in there with him," I answered.

"I'll need a statement from him," said the officer. "Especially if your grandfather and your friend want to press additional charges for forcible confinement."

"What's going to happen to the horses?" I asked.

"Ultimately, I imagine new homes will have to be found for them. For now, they'll be seized by the police."

"How do you seize fifty wild horses?" I said.

The officer scratched his head. "Good question."

I smiled. It didn't really matter—the important thing was that Rosie was free.

chapter nineteen

"Whoa, there. Easy, girl," I said softly. Rosie shifted uneasily, her hooves clattering on the metal floor of the horse trailer. I swung the door open and Rosie snorted, then made her way down the ramp into Grandpa's corral.

"Let her get her bearings." Grandpa folded the ramp and clipped it, then shut the gate to the corral. "We'll bring her some hay later."

I stood on the bottom rail of the fence and watched Rosie explore her new home.

She seemed nervous, but not scared. Her nose lifted to the wind, she trotted around the perimeter of the fence, smelling the new scents.

"I can't believe she's really mine," I told Grandpa.

He slung an arm over my shoulder and we watched Rosie together, her bright coat lit to a fiery red by the late afternoon sun. "We—you, really—have a lot of work ahead of you. Gentling her, breaking her, training her to jump. She's a nice little horse, but you'll have your struggles with her. A rider does with every horse," he said.

"I know." I heaved a happy sigh. "That's okay. After all that we went through, I'm just glad she's really here. It's all over."

Grandpa smiled. "Actually, Reese, it's only just begun."

Acknowledgments

Thanks go to David Poulsen and Jodi Malm for their helpful advice on the general practices involved in shipping animals for meat, and to Sara Compton for allowing me to sit in on riding lessons at Teesdale English Riding School and for letting me "borrow" Grady, one of Teesdale's horses, for a promotional photo. An especially big thank-you is owed to Gigi Morse for sharing her insight and knowledge about show jumping, for inviting me to her horse shows so I could see first-hand what it's like, for reading this manuscript for accuracy, and for her sincere enthusiasm about the writing of this book.

Author's Note

While Reese's story is fictional, the events described in this novel are based on a real incident. On January 25, 1994, a military-sanctioned roundup of over 1,200 feral horses began on Canadian Forces Base Suffield. Those horses were called feral instead of wild because their forebears were originally domesticated horses that escaped or roamed, forming a herd that bred and became untamed. True wild horses have never been tamed, but for the purposes of this story I have referred to them as wild. I have also fictionalized the actual roundup for my story.

The Suffield wild horses roamed the military land for more than fifty years. In the early 1990s, arguments were made that the horses were destroying fragile grasslands, and the roundup began. Animal-rights activists opposed the roundup, fearing that the horses might be mistreated or sold for meat. Although the Canadian military put rules in place to try to protect the horses, there were later allegations that many of the horses, which were supposedly adopted legitimately, were slaughtered for profit. While these allegations were never proven, this scandal was the basis for Reese's story.

More titles in the Orca Sports series

Rebel Glory
by Sigmund Brouwer

ISBN 1-55143-631-0

More titles in the Orca Sports series

All-Star Pride
by Sigmund Brouwer

ISBN 1-55143-635-3

More titles in the Orca Sports series

Tiger Threat
by Sigmund Brouwer

ISBN 1-55143-639-6

Michele Martin Bossley is the author of a number of sports books for young readers. She is also the author of *Swiped* in the Orca Currents series. Michele lives with her family in Calgary, Alberta.